Everything with You

KAYLEE RYAN

To my KAC. You ladies know who you are. Your support means the world to me.

Cover Design: Shanoff Designs
Photographer: Lindee Robinson Photography
Editing: Hot Tree Editing
Formatting: Deaton Author Services

Chapter One

L iam

My eyes are glued to the dance floor as I watch my wife and my sister having the time of their lives. Watching her smile and laugh, damn, I could do this forever. Watching her walk down the aisle with Mr. Emerson, the moment our eyes locked with one another, I swear I felt the world move.

Before she walked down the aisle, I had Aiden, Hales, and my mom and dad deliever her a gift to represent her something old, something new, something borrowed, and something blue. Each gift was a piece of me I was giving her, until she said, "I do." I stood next to the priest, with Aiden to my right, trying to hold it together. I watched as each guest took their seat, idly talking about the decorations. There were flowers of white and purple rimmed in silver surrounding the church and candles along the aisles. My Allie wanted a fairytale wedding and that's what I gave her.

"Hales." I hear Allie's voice, bringing me back to the present. She and Hales are dancing to "Call Me Maybe" and she's happy. We're happy.

Today is my wedding day and my face hurts from smiling. Today, my beautiful girl became my wife. The moment she appeared at the end of the aisle, it took everything I had in me not to run to her. That moment, the moment I laid eyes on my wife, will forever be engrained in my memory. I don't think there will ever be a moment in my life that tops today. I was thrilled when I made it into the League. I knew I would be able to live out my dream with Allie by my side. I thought that was the happiest day of my life; I was wrong. Nothing will top this, ever. I know Aiden is sitting next to me and he is just as enthralled with my sister as I am my wife. We can't even pull our eyes away from them to carry on a conversation. He asked Hales to marry him earlier and, of course, she said yes. My best friend is now officially going to be my brother, Allie's too.

Life is good.

Feeling a strong hand clamp down on my shoulder, I don't bother to turn to see who it is. It doesn't matter. My eyes are glued to my beautiful wife. "What are you two-" my dad's voice trails off as he follows our stare. Aiden and I have been watching them for...well, I really don't know how long. All I know is that I could watch her like this forever. I want that smile to stay plastered on her face.

"Never mind," he says with a chuckle.

The girls walk off toward the restroom and allow me to acknowledge my dad. "She's beautiful," I tell him even though it's unnecessary. My wife is glowing.

Dad laughs and shakes his head at me. He knows I'm a goner; that girl has me wrapped tight.

Aiden turns to us. "She said yes." His smile is beaming.

Dad throws his head back and laughs. "Did you really think she wouldn't?"

"No. I mean yes, I thought she would say yes, but it's official. She's mine, or at least she will be," he tells us. "Hales wants a short engagement, so soon."

Dad smiles at him. "Just remember she was mine first. She will always be my little girl. I'm trusting you with her," he warns. I can see the warmth in his eyes. He knows just as well as I do that Hales is in good hands. Aiden worships her and he should. He fought his attraction to my little sister. He didn't want to ruin our friendship or theirs. All he had to do was tell me she was his, Allison and I knew. He loves her irrevocably. As her brother, that's all I can ask for.

Aiden nods. He doesn't need to say anything; we all know. He loves her and she loves him. Like I said, life is good.

Dad asks us about the season and Aiden and I are officially distracted, that is, until I feel small hands come around my waist. Her scent surrounds me and I immediately place my hands over hers. I feel her rest her head against my back. Gently I pull on her hand to bring her in front of me. She's still in her wedding dress. Her hair is falling around her face from all the dancing. As beautiful as she is in that dress, I want to see it on the floor. I can't wait to get her out of it and make love to her for the first time as my wife.

Pulling her tight against my chest, I lean down and whisper in her ear, "I need to get you out of this dress, my beautiful wife."

Allie blushes and tightens her arms around my waist. She looks up at me with a faint smile. "Liam, we have to cut the cake. We can't leave yet." She gently smacks my chest as to scold me.

I look over her head at the table the cake sits on. "Let's do this," I say, clasping her hand in mine and dragging her to the table. If this damn cake is all that's in my way of ravishing my new wife, it's being sliced, diced, and whatever else you do to a cake. I can't wait much longer.

We reach the table and Allison is laughing. "Liam—" The sound of her laughter warms my heart. She's had so much sadness; she deserves this, all this and more.

I don't give her the chance to say anything else before my lips crash with hers. I hear a throat clearing, and I groan as I force myself to pull my lips from hers. Looking up, I see my mom standing there holding a knife and wearing a smile. "I can only assume you're ready to cut the cake." *Duh? Have you seen my wife?*

I nod. "You can also assume I want my wife to myself, but this cake cutting business is preventing that. So can we move this little tradition along? Please?" I ask her. I bat my eyelashes, trying to come off as sweet as possible. All I need is Mom coming up with another ritual that we have to complete before I can be alone with my wife.

She laughs. I'm glad my family, including my bride, find my need for her so funny. Do they not realize the kind of will power I am using to keep her in that dress? Do they not know how bad I need to make love to her as Allison MacCoy? Shit, my dick strains against the zipper of my monkey suit just thinking about her, Allison MacCoy, my wife.

"Allie, baby, is this the last thing before we can go?" I whisper to her. I want to get her word, so Mom can't sneak something else in on us.

She winks and nods yes. Thank you, Lord above.

I reach for the knife and my mom slaps my hand. "Liam, we have to have it announced so everyone can watch," she scolds me.

I roll my eyes and gesture with my free hand, the one that is not holding my wife tight against me, to get the ball rolling.

With a smile and shaking her head, Mom signals to the DJ and he stops the music to announce the cutting of the cake.

Finally.

iden

Hales and I are on the dance floor. I'm holding her tight in my arms when the DJ stops the music and announces it's time to cut the cake. I laugh at my best friend and future brother-in-law's lack of patience this evening. Liam has grumbled all night how he can't wait to get Allie home. Can't say as I blame him; she is a beautiful bride. I tug my angel a little tighter at the thought of our wedding. Soon, it needs to be soon.

"Good grief, Liam is so damn impatient. All this planning we did and he's just going to whisk her away," Hailey huffs.

I softly chuckle at her annoyance and bring my lips to her ear. "Angel, he wants to make love to his wife. You can bet your sweet ass that I'm going to be the same way, future Mrs. Emerson," I whisper.

I feel her body shiver, and just like that, the subject is dropped. She's said all along that she wants a small intimate wedding, so I hope within the next few days we can nail this shit down and set a date. We fought too long and too hard to be together and I want it to be official. I want her living in my house, the one she helped me pick out. I want her to be the first person I see each morning and the last before I fall asleep. This last year has been tough. We finally worked our shit out to be together, but spent most of our time apart. She needed to finish school and I was busy with my rookie season in the League. I'm tired of waiting. I need this to happen now. I need her to be my wife.

I laugh at Liam and how over-the-top he can be with Allie but I get it. Of course, I have to razz him, but I understand.

Hales grabs my hand and leads me to the table so we are up close and personal with the happy couple. We watch as Liam and Allie cut the cake. Liam gently places a small piece in Allie's mouth. When it's her turn, she smashes it against his face. He immediately reaches for her and places his lips against her. They are now both covered in cake and wearing blinding smiles.

Hales leans up on her tiptoes; I bend down and meet her halfway. Her lips land next to my ear. "Can we do this soon? I'm ready for that to be us," she whispers.

I take her hand and lead her out of the room and down the hall. We step into the room we were in just hours before where I asked her to be my wife. As soon as we enter, she glances up at the ceiling and looks at the stars. "You're amazing," she says, still staring at the night sky I created.

"Angel, you need to understand something," I tell her, leading her to the bench so we can sit. I see worry flash across her face. I lift my hand and cup her cheek, gently caressing her with my thumb. "I would marry you tonight if I thought that is what you really wanted. I'm sure, with the right amount of money, we can get a marriage license and convince the minister to marry us too." She goes to speak and I place my fingers over her lips to stop her. "I don't want to wait either, but I want you to have a wedding that you will always remember. I want you to have your special day. I want you to experience all the excitement that comes with planning a wedding. You know, going shopping for a wedding dress, looking at hundreds of dresses, and us trying the cakes and picking out the invitations." I rub her hands and kiss each knuckle. "These are the memories I want with you, because I'd do anything for you, angel. So let's enjoy the rest of tonight and tomorrow we can sit down, set a date, and start planning. My vote is sooner rather than later, just so you know." Leaning in, my lips brush hers. Soft at first, but when I hear her little moan, I lose it. Moving my tongue with hers, I grab her body and pull her toward me, moving away from the wedding. Finding a chair, I grab her ass and lift her up. Her legs wrap around my waist as I slowly sit down. Fuck, she tastes so good.

I need more of her. I will always need more. Just as I'm about to devour her, we're interrupted by my ringing cell phone. Hales reaches in my pocket and pulls it out, showing me the screen.

Liam. Perfect timing, my man.

"Yes, my dear brother," she says sugary sweet into the phone.

"Hales, where the hell are you two? I finally convinced my wife it's time to go, but she refuses to leave until she says goodbye to the two of you. So you and Aiden need to get to the entrance now," he says, then hangs up, not even bothering to let her respond.

I chuckle. "We better go say goodbye to the happy couple." I kiss her one last time before leading her out the door and leaving our starry night behind.

"Finally." Liam says when he spots us walking toward them. I keep my smartass comments to myself because I hope to be exactly where he is very soon.

He has his arms around Allison and I reach out and tug her away from him. He scowls at me, but I ignore him. I wrap her in a hug. "Be safe and enjoy your honeymoon." I kiss her on the cheek as Hales pulls her from my embrace and into hers.

I walk to stand next to Liam, letting the girls have their moment. "Take care of her," I tell him. I know he will, but it just felt like I needed to say it.

Liam throws his arm over my shoulder. "Always, my man. You do the same." He gestures to Hailey.

"She's in here," I tell him as I place my hand over my chest, just above my heart.

"Then we're on the same page," he says, reaching out to pull Allison back into his arms. Greedy bastard.

Hailey steps back into my arms and I waste no time pulling her against me. "Be safe," she says, her voice cracking. "I love you both and I am so freaking happy for the two of you." She manages to get it out before her tears start to fall. I tighten my hold on her and gently wipe the tears from her cheeks.

Leaning down, I drop a kiss on her temple. "Love you, angel."

Allie pulls Hailey from my arms and gives her another fierce hug. She releases her, promising to send a post card, as Liam lifts her in his arms and carries her out the door to the awaiting limo.

I reach out and tug Hales back into my arms where she belongs. "Soon, angel. I need you to be Hailey Emerson, soon," I say, kissing her lips.

Chapter Three

A llison

Once we're in the limo, and Liam makes sure the privacy screen is up before he crashes his lips to mine. He consumes me with his kiss and I couldn't be happier. This man is my husband. In the eyes of the law, we are a family. A family. Today, my dream of having a family of my own came true, well, half of it. I want to be a mom. I want to carry Liam's baby and give our child the world, just like my parents. Thinking about them makes me smile. I know they were with me today, and I know my dad was walking next to me as I walked to my prince. My Liam. Everything I want came true in a few hours. But now I want more. I want to give Liam a gift, a gift no one else will ever give him. I want more than anything for us to expand our family.

But I don't know if this is what Liam wants. He's doing so well in the League and his dreams are coming true. I want to be there for him and support him. So for now, I'll be quiet until the time's right. I've been avoiding the topic. I just haven't found the right time to bring it up. He knows I want kids, a family of our own, and he's on board with that. However, now that we're married, I don't want to wait to start. I don't know how Liam will take it. He's so new in his career; I don't know if he's ready. I understand if he's not and I'll wait. We're young, but I can't deny I would be disappointed.

Liam plays with my hair, nuzzling his nose in my neck, whispering how much he loves me. "How are you feeling, Mrs. MacCoy?"

"Perfect, Mr. MacCoy."

We're staying at our house before flying to Tahiti tomorrow afternoon. Liam insisted we have the first night to ourselves, and, well, who am I to argue with him. Throughout the wedding, all I could think about was letting him take me and love me all over. Tonight will be our first night together as husband and wife. Wow, I'm a wife. I'm Liam MacCoy's wife. And tonight I get to show him how much I love him. His fingers run along my bare shoulders down my arms. "Liam," I mumble.

"Yes?"

I sigh, "You have to wait."

"Consider this foreplay, Mrs. MacCoy, and as soon as I get you in the house, I'm making you mine. I'm going to spend hours reacquainting myself with your body and cherishing every inch."

I shiver to his words and touch. It was just as hard for me as it was for him to not disappear and consummate our marriage, but family is important. He is now officially mine and I wanted to bask in that. It's been a long time for me and I just wanted to be in the moment. I knew we were going to have tonight. Silly man, he knows how he affects me.

I find it over-the-top how we have a limo drive us home, but Liam said there was no way he would be able to concentrate on driving knowing that he was minutes away from making love to his wife for the first time. Again, how do I argue with that?

During the drive home, Liam's lips barely leave mine. His hands, gentle yet demanding, roam my body. "I can't wait to strip you out of this," he whispers as his hands find their way under my dress.

We are so wrapped up in the moment, it takes the limo driver knocking on our window for us to even realize we're already home.

Pulling away and rest his forehead against mine. "I love you, my beautiful wife," he whispers and places one more soft kiss on my lips.

He steps out of the limo and reaches his hand out for me. My feet barely hit the ground before he sweeps me into his arms and carries me to the front door. The limo driver is there smiling and holding the door open with a smirk on his face. "Have a good evening, Mr. and Mrs. MacCoy." My heart thunders against my chest at the sound of my new name.

This is real.

This is my life.

Liam kicks the door closed with his foot and continues to carry me to our room. I see a soft glow filter from the hallway. Gently sits me on the edge of the bed and steps away. My eyes filter across the room, taking it all in. The soft glow is candles, too many to count. Liam has turned our bedroom into romantic bliss. I don't bother asking how he pulled it off. The lengths this man goes through to show his love for me is without bounds.

I reach out for him and he doesn't hesitate. He moves his large frame to stand between my legs. My eyes find his, and the passion and love I see is strong enough to have brought me to my knees if I were standing. Liam moves closer as I wrap my arms around his waist and hold him next to me. My head is resting against his chest and I feel his heartbeat, the steady rise and fall with each breath. I can't wait anymore; I need him. I run my hands up his chest and stop when I reach his collar. I begin to unbutton his shirt. My eyes find his once again and neither one of us can look away. I want to memorize this, all of it.

Once I have his shirt unbuttoned, Liam laces his fingers through mine and gently pulls me so I am standing in front of him. He trails kisses down my neck, causing me to burn with need for him. Running his tongue across my shoulder, he spins me so my back is now facing him. His lips find the back of my neck as he releases the zipper of my dress. The tight bodice loosens, and I know all I need to do is shimmy my hips and the dress will fall away. So, I do.

My husband growls in my ear, spins me around, and crashes his lips with mine. I guess he likes my secret, well, Victoria's Secret. My barely there, white, sheer thong and strapless bra are all that remain. It seems he approves.

"Mrs. MacCoy, will you do me the honor of allowing me to make love to you," he whispers in my ear.

I melt at his sweet request. My heart is no longer mine. This is not a new revelation, but in this moment, it's reconfirmed. Liam MacCoy, my husband, owns me.

"Please," is all I can get out before his lips mold to mine.

Chapter Four

H^{ailey}

Aiden and I hang around the reception for a little longer. I want nothing more than to take him home so we can celebrate our engagement. My mom, however, has other plans. She and Aiden's mom found us as soon as Liam and Allie left and have been talking wedding nonstop. Don't get me wrong, I love them both and I want them to be a part of the planning, but I don't want big. I just want Aiden. A small, intimate wedding is what I want, and my fiancé has promised that's what we will have. So as I listen to our mothers getting their hopes up, I start to worry over my decision. I hate to upset them tonight and ruin the evening. Aiden, always in tune with me, stands and bends to whisper in my ear, "Dance with me, angel."

I sigh with relief that I have an escape from the extravagant wedding talk. Aiden leads me to the dance floor, our fingers tightly laced. Reaching a dark corner, he twirls me around so we are chest to chest. His strong arms wrap around my waist as I place my hands behind his neck. Aiden buries his face in my neck and breathes me in.

We stay that way for the remainder of the song and all of the next. Once the beat of the third picks up, Aiden lifts his head and kisses me. His lips are soft yet firm. I open for him and he doesn't hesitate for a taste. Way too soon for my liking, the kiss ends and I'm breathless. This is normal; Aiden always leaves me breathless.

Resting his forehead against mine, he says, "Baby, I want you to have your day. I want it to be what you've dreamed of. All I ask is that we do it soon." It's as if he can read my mind.

Just like that, the stress over disappointing our mothers is gone. This is about me and Aiden. The life we want to build together. Our day. The day we promise to love and cherish each other until death do us part. Not that it will take the vows to solidify what we have. My love for him his has no bounds.

"Take me home," I say.

Without question, he leads me back to our parents, and with a round of hugs and congratulations we say goodbye.

The silence of the drive is comfortable. Aiden had his hand on my thigh and I'm gently running my fingers through his hair as he drives us home. Every once in a while, he will glance over at me and smile. I love this man. My mind wonders to how hard we fought against this pull that we have with one another. We spent so much wasted time worrying about what others would think. What we should have been doing was loving each other.

Out of nowhere, it hits me. I know what I want. How I want to promise myself to him. "I want to get married on the beach, at night, under the stars. I don't care where we go. I just want it to be soon. Liam and Allie will be back this time next week." I want this. No more waiting, no more should we or shouldn't we. I don't want to wait to spend the rest of my life with him. I twist my new engagement ring on my finger, and I can't prevent the smile that breaks out across my face as it sparkles in the moonlight. "I just want to be your wife," I say, my voice soft.

Aiden pulls into his driveway, turns off the ignition, and adjusts his body to face me. He reaches over and tucks my unruly hair behind my ear. I can only imagine how it looks after Allie and I danced all night. His thumb gently traces my cheek. Leaning in, he whispers, "Angel, that sounds perfect," and his lips find mine. He takes his time, allowing us to savor one another.

As soon as we're inside, I kick off one heel and then the other. My feet are killing me. I reach my arm up behind my neck trying to grasp the zipper of my dress, not having much luck. I hear Aiden chuckle, and then his hands replace mine. He slowly releases my zipper while following the path with his lips. I shiver at the contact.

"Are you cold, angel?" His breath is hot against my ear.

I don't bother to respond to him. He knows I'm not cold. He knows how he affects me, how my body responds to his lips against my skin.

Aiden begins a path from my ear to my collarbone with his tongue. I tilt my head to the side allowing him full access. His lips trail back up to my ear as he places his hands on my shoulders and slowly slips my dress off my arms. "I want to make love to my fiancé," He speaks against my ear, his voice thick with desire.

I turn to face him, all the while trying to wiggle free of my dress. As soon as it falls to the floor, I jump in his arms. His hands immediately cup my ass and I wrap my legs around his waist. I bring his lips to mine and take what I want.

Aiden.

My Aiden.

His tongue meets mine stroke for stroke as he carries me to his room. As he flops me down on the bed and begins to crawl up my body, it hits me.

Aiden is mine, forever mine. We're getting married.

Chapter Five

L iam

If I would have known what Allison had on underneath this dress, there is no way in hell I would have stayed at the reception that long. The sheer material that she calls a bra and panties is barely there. I walk her back toward the bed until her legs hit the mattress. I place my hands on her hips and dip my head to kiss her lips. I take my time. I want this night to be memorable for both of us. This is the first time I will make love to her as my wife. If I wasn't so fucking turned on right now, I might be nervous. I slow the kiss and I hear a groan of protest slip from her lips. I smile, my wife is ready for me.

Tightening my grip on her hips, I lift her off her feet and toss her on the bed. She giggles as she falls into the soft mattress. Her hair is fanned out across the pillows and her eyes shine with love. I just about lose my shit just from looking at her. A slow smile spreads across my face at the thought of seeing her this way every day for the rest of my life. I am one lucky son of a bitch.

Allie reaches out and grasps my hand. "Make love to me, husband," she whispers.

Her words spring me into action. I fumble with my zipper as I tear out of my clothes. Allison's eyes follow my every move. I can see the hunger in her eyes. She sits up and removes her bra, tossing it across the room. She lies back on the bed and lifts her hips. I reach up and slide her poor excuse for panties down her legs, tossing them over my shoulder. Not able to wait another minute, I climb on the bed and bring my body over hers. I rest my hands beside her head, holding my weight. I lean down and kiss her neck. Starting at her collarbone and working my way up to her ear, I nip her gently and soothe the spot with my tongue. It's then that I whisper, "Every day for the rest of my life, Mrs. MacCoy." She shivers at my words. I settle myself against her and gently grind my hips into her heat. I can feel she's ready for me. My wife anchors her legs around me, which causes me to slip inside of her.

I suck in a breath at the contact. In reality, I know this isn't really different. I've been inside of her more times than I can count. Every single time she takes my breath away, but to me it feels different. Maybe it's the caveman in me; I don't really know. What I do know is that nothing has ever felt like this. My heart is pounding in my chest and I can feel my body tremble. Finally, she is finally mine.

I lean down and rest my forehead against hers. "Beautiful," I say softly. My voice is gruff with the emotion of the moment.

I feel her fingers running through my hair. "I didn't think it could get any better," she whispers.

I lift my eyes to hers and I see a blush cross her face. We are so in tune with each other it's scary. "I will love you until I take my last breath," I say as I begin to move and make love to my wife.

Our lovemaking is slow as we savor the moment. My hands roam her body as I continue to push in and out of her. Our eyes meet and neither one of us look away. The intensity of her eyes on me has me picking up speed. Gentle yet firm thrusts. I can feel her tighten around me and she closes her eyes as she falls over the edge. Watching my wife come undone has me right behind her as I let go, calling her name.

After I catch my breath, I lift myself to move off of her. Her arms wrap around me and hold me close. "Don't go. I just...don't move, please," she asks.

Never one to deny her anything, I stay put, lean down and kiss her. My tongue traces her lips. I'm holding my weight on my arms, so I don't crush her. As our kiss gets heated, I flip us over, never breaking the connection between us, putting her on top of me. Placing my hand on the back of her head, I hold her lips against mine, tasting her, taking what's mine.

Allie breaks this kiss and pulls her body up into a sitting position. Reaching out, I tuck her hair behind her ear. I cup her face with my palm. "I love you, Allison MacCoy."

Her face lights up with a beautiful smile as she rocks her hips. Just like that, I'm ready to go again. This time my wife takes control.

Chapter Six

 iden

Touching her hair, watching her sleep, these are the moments I love. Her face is peaceful and her lips part a little. Soft snores come out of her sexy nose. Her hand moves to mine and she holds it tight. Even in her sleep she reaches out for me. Damn, I fucking love this girl. Waking up with Hailey in my arms is something that doesn't happen enough for my liking. With me being so busy during the season, it seems as though the weekends that nursing school did not have her tied down were the weekends I had away games. Hailey used the time to focus on volunteering at the hospital. As a part of her clinicals, she needed to choose an area she was interested in. I can still remember the day she finally decided. She called me and I could hear the excitement in her voice. That was the day she did her first rotation for labor and delivery. She immediately fell in love with witnessing new life and she was hooked.

Even though I hated being away from her, it was worth it to watch her make her dreams come true. She graduated from nursing school just a few shorts weeks ago. She's now a Registered Nurse and I am so fucking proud of her. I've waited patiently, and now that she is through school, I need for her to be here with me. I bought this house for us. I hate being here without her.

My hand that is resting on her belly pulls her tighter against my chest. I can't find the words to explain how it feels to have her in my arms like this, skin to skin, tight against me. This is heaven. I need this every day for the rest of my life. I know she said yes, but we have spent so much time waiting. I need her now, permanently. Our conversation last night about our wedding runs through my mind. Today, my beautiful fiancé is going to pick a date and a destination.

Hailey wiggles her hips and I chuckle softly against her ear. "Good morning, angel."

"Hmmm," is her reply. She rolls over and places her lips against my chest. Wrapping my arms around her, I decide now is as good of a time as any to start wearing her down about moving in. If she says we have to wait until we're married, I'm buying tickets to Vegas tonight.

"Let's stay in bed forever, Aiden."

"We have a lot to do today." I'm gently rubbing my hands up and down her back as she burrows further into me. "We need to pick a date and a destination. We also need to start packing up your things and get you settled in here." I decide to just put it out there and not really give her the option. I hold my breath, waiting for her to shoot me down.

"Sounds like I need to get motivated. We better hop to it," she replies as she jumps out of bed and heads to the bathroom. I hear the shower turn on. I'm stunned. No fight, no back and forth, just acceptance.

I don't know how long I've sat here, letting her response sink in, but it was long enough for Hailey to finish her shower. She struts out of the bathroom fully clothed. She stops in front of me where I sit on the side of the bed and kisses me. "I'll go make breakfast, while you shower." Then she turns and walks to the door. Reaching the door, she turns to face me. "Get your ass in gear, Emerson. We got things to do today." She winks and saunters out of the bedroom.

Well, all right then. I hop off the bed and make quick work of showering and getting dressed. I find Hailey in the kitchen eating an omelet and toast. There is a plate with a larger portion of the same sitting next to her. She has my laptop open and is intently reading as she shovels in her breakfast.

"What ya looking at?" I ask around a mouthful of food.

"Destinations. I found one. Do you want to see?" she asks.

"Yes, but I don't really care where it is as long as it's your dream location. All I want is for you to be my wife," I tell her. I know it makes me sound like an asshole, but I can't make myself care. It doesn't matter when or where I marry her. As long as she becomes Hailey Emerson, I'm a happy man.

She turns the computer screen and shows me a picture of a white sandy beach, water so clear you see everything below, and clear blue skies. "This," she says, pointing her fork at the screen, "is Pink Sands Beach at Harbour Island in the Bahamas. It's perfect," she says as she shovels in another bite of her omelet.

I study the screen. "Are there any nighttime photos?" She did say she wanted to get married under the stars.

Hailey clicks the mouse and the next picture is the same as before only the night sky is filled with thousands of bright stars. "Yes, but I think maybe sunset might be better and we can celebrate into the night. Dance for the first time under the stars." She watches me as I absorb her words. She chews on her bottom lip...waiting.

I gulp down my orange juice and lean into her. I place my hand on the back of her head and bring her lips close to mine. "How soon can we make this happen? It sounds amazing." I kiss her because I just can't not. This girl owns me.

Pulling back from the kiss, she moans and I can't help but chuckle. I love this, having her here, having this time together. "Well, we need a guest list. I kind of want it small, you know?"

I carry our plates to the counter and load them in the dishwasher. "I agree; besides, the fewer people involved, the faster we can make this happen."

"So our parents, and I was really thinking just Allie and Liam. What do you think?" she asks me.

I reach into my pocket and pull out my Am Ex. I place the card in her hand and wrap her fingers around it. I drop to my knees in front of her. "Make it happen, angel. Anything you want. I think it all sounds perfect and the sooner the better." I kiss her quickly and head back to the dishwasher to finish loading.

Chapter Seven

A llison

The flight to Tahiti was exhausting. Of course, our day started off bad when Liam and I overslept. We almost missed our plane. My husband called the airport and used his newfound celebrity status to delay enough for us to rush through security and board our flight. I hate to rush and being late for anything, but as thoughts of last night flood my mind, I have no regrets. Our first night as husband and wife exceeded my expectations.

Thank goodness we already had our bags packed. We have one suitcase between the two of us. Liam tried to argue how all we needed was a carry on. We will be there for seven days. When I debated, his reasoning was he plans to keep me naked and in bed, that clothes would not be needed. I didn't argue after that. Seven days in bed with the hotness that is my husband sounds like heaven to me. Our overwater suite is amazing. It's a new experience for both of us, the first of many.

"What do you think, beautiful girl?" Liam places his arms around my waist as we stand out on the deck and watch the sun setting over the water.

I lean my head back against his shoulder. "It's amazing. I don't think I've seen anything this beautiful," I say, turning my face so I can see him.

His eyes lock on mine. "I have," he replies as his lips find mine. I turn in his arms and indulge in the moment. We are newlyweds after all.

Liam hugs me tight to his chest. "This is amazing, being here with you, my wife. No distractions..." He trails off. It doesn't matter, because I know exactly what he's thinking. I feel it too. This is paradise and not just the location.

Liam's stomach growls. "Let's call the resort and have them deliver dinner. I'm not ready to share you with the public. Besides, the longer we stay hidden, the better chance we have of the paparazzi not finding out we are here. I know the resort is known for its high security, but I just don't want to deal with it yet."

"Sounds like a plan. Just order me whatever; you know what I like. I'm going to go freshen up a little." I turn to enter our suite and feel his large hand smack my ass. I whip my head around. He's wearing a sexy smirk as he shrugs and follows me inside.

After a quick shower, one that my husband deemed necessary to join, I brush out my hair and decide to just tie it up on top of my head. I slip into one of Liam's T-shirts and call it good. I hear the knock on the door; good, the food is here and I'm starving. As I walk into the room, I remember I haven't taken my birth control pill today. I head back into the bathroom and dig through our bag of toiletries. I know I put them in here. I'm starting to panic. Liam and I have not yet talked about when we would start a family and I don't want him to think I tricked him into it. This is something that we should decide together. I dump the bag onto the counter and sift through the contents. This is how Liam finds me when he comes to tell me the food is here.

"What are you doing, baby?" he tilts his head to the side, watching me.

"Where are they?" I mutter to myself.

Liam steps into the room. "What are you looking for, beautiful?" he asks.

I lift my head and blow the bangs out of my eyes. "My birth control pills. I know I put them in here yesterday after I packed. I cannot find them anywhere. Have you seen them?" I ask him as I continue searching the pockets of our bag again.

Without a word Liam grabs my hips and sets me on the counter. I open my legs and he stands between them. Both of his hands caress my cheeks. "You didn't lose them, beautiful girl," he says gently.

I release the breath I was holding. "Thank the Lord," I say.

He studies me. "I thought you wanted to make a baby with me?" he asks. I can hear the insecurity in his voice.

Whoa, what? Liam wants a baby...Now? "I do. I want that more than anything, but we haven't talked about it and I didn't want to just assume," I explain.

He continues to watch me, his big, strong hands still holding onto my cheeks. He releases my face and wraps his arms around me in a hug. His lips nip at my ear. "I threw them away," he whispers so softly I almost don't even hear him.

He pulls away and watches me, waiting for my reaction. "Did you just say you...threw them away?" I ask. I try to hold in my smile until I know for sure that is what he really said. My palms are sweaty and my heart is racing as I wait for him to confirm or deny if I'm losing my mind.

"Yep." He pops the p and shrugs. "I thought that was the plan. Get married, make lots of babies, and love you unconditionally for the rest of my life?"

"Lots of babies?" I laugh, watching the smile on his face.

His arms go wide. "I want a football team of boys, and little girls who'll keep me up at night, so remind me to get my gun permit." I love the excitement in his eyes. I can hear it in his voice. Liam wants this. He wants a family. "Besides," he comes closer to me, kissing my lips, "the more kids we have means more sexy time with my wife."

I can no longer hold back the smile I know is plastered across my face. "Squeee." I jump from the counter and into Liam's arms. I lock my legs around his waist and kiss him. I feel his chest rumble with laughter. I release his lips and lean back a little. "So we're really gonna start trying?" I ask, needing to hear him say it again.

Liam smiles and carries me to the bed. His sits down with me still locked around him like a monkey. He has one hand on my back to keep me from falling and the other slips under his shirt, and rests it on my belly. "I love you, Allison. I love the life we have planned. The thought of part of me growing inside of you..." He swallows. His eyes never leaving mine. "I can't wait to make babies with you. To watch your body change and grow. To meet the little miracle that is created out of the love we share for one another. It's my dream too."

There are tears running down my cheeks. I untangle my body from his and stand up. I lift his shirt over my head, which leaves me standing before him in nothing but my smile. I step between his legs and push on his chest until he is lying back on the bed. My hands find the waist of his gym shorts and he lifts his hips automatically so I can rid him of them. We are now exactly how Liam said we would be, no clothes, nothing between us. I climb up on the bed and straddle his hips.

Our food is just going to have to wait.

Chapter Eight

H ailey

As Aiden finishes the dishes, I pick up my phone and call the travel agency. I make flight reservations for the eight of us as well as room reservations. Aiden and I will stay in a private villa while the others each have a suite at the resort. I don't bother calling to see if they can make it. I know they will. All six of them would drop anything to be there with us. That is why I want only them. They are the most important people in our lives and it seems right to share this with just them. To have them be a part of our day.

The travel agency puts me in contact with the resort. Lucky for me, they have a wedding planner. I speak to her about the simplicity and how I want to say our vows at sunset. We talk small floral arrangements, and she assures me that our date of three weeks is more than enough time to make it happen. We talk for a few more minutes and hang up with the promise to talk again in the next few days to touch base.

I walk to the counter where Aiden is leaning against the sink with his legs crossed at the ankles. I slip my hand in his back pocket and pull out his wallet. I place his Am Ex back in its slot and return his wallet. I reach up and run my fingers through his hair at the nape of his neck. "Well, Mr. Emerson, is appears that three weeks from today, you will be a married man."

I feel his arms come around me as he crushes me to his chest. "Three fucking weeks and you're mine," he whispers in my ear, holding me tight. Then out of nowhere, "Hell yeah." he shouts as he lifts me off the ground and twirls me in circles.

He finally stops spinning us with my back to the counter. He places his arms on either side, caging me in. "I love you, angel."

"I love you too, Aiden Emerson." I place my hands on his hips and tug his body closer. "It seems as though there was one more item on that to-do list. I can't for the life of me figure it out. Maybe it will come to me on the drive home." I know I'm ruffling his feathers. It's fun to watch after all the time we spent fighting being together and then the distance with me finishing school. I know he wants me here.

"You are home," he growls. "We are driving to your condo and we are not leaving until everything you want is packed up and brought here. This is our home, angel." His voice is almost pleading for me to agree.

"That's right. You mentioned something about me moving in," I tease him. I know it's cruel to torture him, but I just can't help it.

"Hailey, baby, don't do that. You know I want you here. I bought this house for us. I need you here. I need your stuff here. I need you," he says. His eyes are pleading with me to say the words he wants to hear.

I decide to put him out of his misery as I smile up at him. "Don't worry, Emerson, I already called Mom and Dad. They have been saving boxes for me for weeks now. They're going to meet us there at three to help us pack everything up."

"Weeks?" he asks.

"Yeah, I mean, you've told me before that you wanted me here with you. I thought it was always the plan once I finished school?"

"It was...it is. I just...I expected you to fight me on it and now I learn that you were planning for it." He leans down and kisses me. His tongue traces my bottom lip before he pulls away.

"Wait a minute. That means we don't have to leave until around noon." He looks at the clock on the stove. "It's only ten o'clock. What-ever will we do for two hours here in our home all alone, my beautiful fiancée?" He wags his eyebrows at me.

I laugh. "Actually, I thought we could head there now. I already have some boxes I had packed up. We can get them loaded and out of the way to give us some more room. It's going to be hard to leave that place behind. It holds a lot of special memories for me."

"Yeah, it really does. But you can go back whenever you want."

"What do you mean? I can go back whenever I want?" I ask. Is he telling me I can leave him? What the hell?

"Calm down, angel. What I mean is that Liam and I talked about it and we're keeping the condo and the furniture for when we visit our folks. That way if we need or want our privacy, we'll have it," he explains.

I lean up on my tiptoes. "Even better. Let's get a move on, Mr. Emerson. I have a fiancé to move in with," I say, smacking him on the ass and running from the room with Aiden hot on my tail.

Chapter Nine

L iam

The sun is starting to rise as the darkness of night fades away. I'm lying on my side propped up on my elbow while my other hand rests on Allie's belly. I can't wait to see her body grow and change with pregnancy. Just the thought that a part of me could already be growing inside of her fills my heart with joy. This woman, my wife, she's turned me into a jumbled ball of emotions. I can't even find the words to explain what she means to me. I catch a lot of shit for it in the locker room. Aiden and I both do. I couldn't care less. At the end of the day, I come home to my beautiful girl and that's all that matters to me.

Allie's hand on my face brings me out of my trance. "Morning," she says in her sleepy, sexy as hell voice.

Leaning down, I place a kiss on her forehead. "Morning, baby." This past week has been incredible.

Allie rolls over as I lie flat on my back. She rests her head against my chest. "What time is it?" she mumbles.

I run my fingers through her hair. "It's just after six. We have to leave for the airport soon," I tell her.

"Mmmm. Were you going to wake me up?" she questions me.

My hand finds its way to her back as I trace her spine. "Yeah, I was just watching you sleep for a few."

Allison lifts her head and rests her chin on my chest, her eyes finding mine. "I loved our time here. I'll miss our little bubble, but I can't wait to get back home."

"We'll have to come back here for an anniversary." My hand stills as she sits up. The sheet drops, revealing her full naked breasts. You would think I would be sated after the week we've had...I'm not. I will never get enough of her. Never.

"I'm going to take a quick shower." Climbing out of bed, she sashays her fine ass into the bathroom. I call and order us breakfast so we can scarf it down before we leave for the airport. I order all of Allie's favorites. She's still in the shower. I decide she needs help. What would happen if she missed a spot?

Throwing the covers off, I make my way to the bathroom. As I open the door, steam hits me in the face. My girl loves her hot showers. Thankful for my nakedness, I slide open the shower door and step in behind her. My hands find her waist and she immediately leans back against my chest. The feel of her soft, wet skin is heaven.

"I was hoping you might join me," she says as I wrap my arms around her waist and bury my face in her neck. The hot water is beating down against my skin, but I don't feel it. All I feel is her. My wife.

Our shower took longer than expected, which caused us to devour our breakfast. Lucky for me, my wife keeps me grounded. She insisted that we pack the majority of our things last night so we wouldn't have to mess with it this morning. She saved our ass. Not that I would be disappointed to spend another day in paradise with her, but I also missed home. I'm ready to live life with my wife, get things back to normal. Well, our new normal anyway. With any luck, my girl is already growing a new member of the MacCoy clan. Let the adventure begin.

As the limo driver pulls into the drive, I hop out and rush to the other side. I know I already carried her over the threshold, but that was a week ago. Today we truly begin the rest of our lives as husband and wife.

Paradise is behind us, but the memories we created there, and maybe a little something else, will be with us forever.

I lean down and scoop Allie up in my arms. She throws her head back in laughter. "Liam, what in the hell are you doing?" she sputters through her laughs. "Didn't we already do this?" she manages to ask.

Leaning down, I kiss her forehead. "Yes, my beautiful wife, we did. However, this is the first day of living our day to day lives as husband and wife, no paradise. We have to start it off right." I wink at her for good measure.

Allie just laughs and allows me to carry her up the steps and through the front door. Luckily, I had this all worked out with our driver so I didn't have to screw around with the door. I made sure he was highly compensated for his door unlocking and holding services.

Once inside, I hear the sound of the door closing. Good man, he follows orders well. I carry my wife into the kitchen and sit her on the island. She spreads her legs for me and I push my frame to stand in between them. I take her face in both of my hands and pull her lips to mine. "This is our forever, beautiful girl," I say, just before I lavish her with kisses.

Chapter Ten

iden

Having Hailey living with me full-time fucking kicks ass. I've been begging her for months to move in and she always fought me. I know she just wanted to focus on school and getting her education. Becoming a nurse was important to her. I'm glad I got to watch her dream come true. I can see her eyes light up when she talks about her work. She doesn't have to work, but she wants to. If I had it my way, she would travel with me everywhere I go. Attached at the hip we would be. I know that's not ideal, but, God, I miss her when I'm away.

We talked the other night about her next step. She applied for a part-time position at the local hospital for labor and delivery. She admitted it will be nice to work for the enjoyment and not because she needs the money to survive. Too many people end up hating the fields they love due to stress and money issues. This will not be the case for my angel. She will not have to worry about how many hours she has or how she is going to come up with next month's rent. She gets to enjoy the job. I couldn't be happier that I'm able to provide for her, for us, so she can enjoy her dream job. I love football and I'm paid well to play. We're living the dream.

"Aiden." she yells down the stairs

"Yeah, babe?" I yell back. Did I mention I love this, living with her?

"Allie just called and wants to know if we want to come over for dinner?" she responds.

"I'm down for whatever, angel. Let me know what you decide." Yes, I'm whipped and damn proud of the fact. I fought to have her and I'm going to do everything in my power to make her happy.

"We leave in an hour," she yells back.

An hour gives me plenty of time to seduce her. I have never been able to keep my hands off of her, but now that she lives here and we are getting married in just over a week, my need for her has reached an all-time high. Lucky for me, my girl feels the same way. Living together is fucking fantastic.

Turning off the TV and tossing the remote on the couch, I bound my way up the steps two at a time. I begin the search for my beautiful fiancée. I thought I would find her in the bedroom, and I did, just not ours. Hailey is in one of our spare bedrooms bent over with her ass in the air. I have no idea what she's doing, and I'm not about to ask her. I need to make sure I send her on a shopping spree to buy more of those pants. I think she calls them yoga pants. Definitely gonna need a few more pair of those.

I watch as she continues to twist and turn the new rug she bought the other day until she gets it right where she wants it. Before she has time to stand back up, I ease in behind her and place my hard length against her ass. I have her right where I want her.

Instead of whining or telling me we don't have time, the little vixen wiggles her fine ass into my crotch. I thought I was hard before, now I'm steel. Bracing my hands on her hips, I grab ahold of her yoga pants and tug. Once I have them at her knees, I place my hand on the small of her back to keep her in that position. I need her in that positon.

With one hand, I work my basketball shorts over my hips and waste no time filling her. She meets each thrust and I feel her tightening around my cock. Fuck, this feels so good. Hailey moans and pushes back against me. Holy shit. I'm not going to last long if she keeps that up. I snake my hand around her. I need to help her get there, because I'm so fucking close. My fingers find her throbbing clit. Playing with her, she screams my name, wanting more. Gripping her hip with my other hand, I fuck her hard and fast. The sounds of our combined moans and our bodies as they meet mesh together and echo throughout the room. "I'm there, angel. Are you with me?" I pant. I hope to hell she is, because I can't hold off much longer.

"Aiden...I...don't stop...I...AHHH." I feel her tighten around me and let go. I hate condoms. I would love nothing more than to feel her with nothing between us as I spill over inside of her. My dick twitches at the thought. Hales has yet to get on birth control and I don't want to push her. I don't mind condoms really; I just want to feel her. It's something that neither one of us has ever done. Ever felt. My heart races at the fact that she's going to be my wife. It's another first that we will experience together.

I slowly pull away from her and lift her in my arms. I settle us onto the bed and just hold her. "I love you, angel," I whisper in her ear.

She's quiet for a long time before she leans up and kisses me softly. "I love you, too. Now get your fine ass in gear or we're going to be late." She smacks my ass and jumps off the bed.

I fucking love this girl.

Chapter Eleven

A llison

Life as husband and wife is not really that much different. Our titles have changed, but that's about it. Liam and I were already living together. There is one difference that I try not to think about. I no longer take my daily dose of birth control. Liam has been making a big deal out of "making a baby" any time he's in the mood. For example, I was running the vacuum the other day and found myself lifted in the air and tossed on the couch. My clothes were quickly removed and he was inside of me. His reasoning was I looked really hot and he was so turned on that he was sure his orgasm would release strong swimmers that could get the job done.

I can't help but laugh at his antics. This silly, crazy, sexy man loves me and wants to make babies with me. I'm all in, no excuses needed, but they are rather entertaining.

"Who was on the phone, babe?" Liam asks me as he walks into the kitchen.

"I called Hales and Aiden to see if they want to come over for dinner." I point to the huge pot on the stove. "I made this huge pot of chili." I don't need to say any more. Liam and Aiden both loved my chili. The pot will be gone before the end of the night. I didn't even tell Hales what we were having. It doesn't really matter, though. We take any reason for the four of us to get together.

"You didn't need to tell me what you were brewing up in here. I can smell your chili from miles away." Liam walks over to the stove, pulls out the silverware drawer, and grabs a spoon. Just as he's about to dip it into the pot, I smack his hand.

"I don't think so, mister. Ace and Hales will be here in half hour or so. You can wait," I scold him. It takes all I have not to laugh at his expression. He pops out his bottom lip and pouts.

"Baby, I love your chili and I'm starving. How am I supposed to smell this fucking kickass creation when my belly is rumbling? I might starve to death before they get here," he whines, laying it on thick.

I bust out laughing at his antics. "Fine, you can taste it you big baby, but no double dipping. I'm going upstairs to change," I say, kissing him on the cheek.

As I walk away, I hear cabinets open and then another drawer. I turn to look over my shoulder and see Liam with a bowl of steaming chili in his hands and a smile on his face. It doesn't take much to make my husband happy.

It takes longer than I thought it would to get ready. I ended up folding a load of laundry and starting another. I have no idea how two people can go through so much laundry. I mentioned this to Liam the other day. Of course, my husband's answer to this was I should throw away all of my clothes and we could live naked ever after. Crazy man.

I make it back downstairs just as Aiden and Hailey knock on the door. I'm not sure why they actually knocked. They have a key and know they are more than welcome to come and go as they please. Hell, they didn't even wait for us to answer; they just waltzed in.

"What's up with knocking?" Liam asks as he gives Hales a hug.

"Just wanted to alert our presence to the newlyweds," Hailey chirps while raising her eyebrows up and down. She looks ridiculous and we all laugh at her. She knows she does, that's why she does it.

"So what's for dinner?" Aiden asks as he puts his arm around my shoulders and pulls me in for a hug.

"She made her chili, man," Liam responds before I get the chance.

"Hell, yeah." Aiden releases me and follows Liam to the kitchen.

"I haven't made the peanut butter sandwiches," I yell at their retreating backs. My words fall on deaf ears as their noses and bellies lead them toward the kitchen.

Hailey and I just laugh at our boys as we follow them to the kitchen. Liam and Aiden both already have a bowl, Liam's second I might add, by the time we get there. Hailey begins making the peanut butter sandwiches while I place the crackers and cheese on the island.

Once we have everything set up, we both make us a bowl and take a place at the table. Liam and Aiden are both leaning against the island. I'm sure they are both about finished with their bowls and will be going back for more.

"So, how's married life?" Hailey asks.

Liam, with his mouthful, replies, "Fucking amazing." then goes back to eating.

I laugh at him. "Babe, I think she was asking me," I tell him.

Liam just shrugs and refills his bowl. This time he tops it with cheese and crackers and grabs two peanut butter sandwiches and takes a seat next to me at the table. Aiden shuffles into the seat next to Hales, his bowl mirroring Liam's.

I turn my attention back to Hailey. "It's really not much different. My name is changed and I can now refer to Liam as my husband, but other than that, it's business as usual," I tell her.

"Not everything is the same, beautiful girl," Liam says. His voice softer, maybe it's because his mouth isn't full this time.

Hailey turns to look at her brother. "Enlighten me, big brother. How has married life changed?" she asks him. She really does seem curious to know. I can only assume she's eager to see if she can place her and Aiden in our shoes.

Liam looks at me and smirks. I brace myself because I know he's about to drop the baby making bombshell on them. We haven't really discussed if we were going to tell people, but this is Aiden and Hailey. "We weren't trying to make a baby before, and now we are." He shoves another spoonful of chili into his mouth as if he didn't just shock the hell out of them.

Hailey coughs around the bite she just took and Aiden grins around his spoon. They both know this is what we wanted. I can only guess they didn't think we would try this soon.

Hailey opens her mouth to speak and Liam cuts her off. "Life is too short; we want a family. We have the means to care for one." He reaches over and grabs my hand and pulls it to his lips. "Besides," he winks at me before looking back across the table at them, "working toward the end goal is a hell of a lot of fun." He smirks.

Chapter Twelve

H ailey

Liam's words cause me to choke on the bite I just took. Holy shit. I know Allison wants kids and Liam does too, but I thought they would wait a while. My big brother is going to be a dad. "I'm going to be an aunt," I blurt out. Wow, Allison is only twenty and Liam just finished his first year in the League. I just assumed they would want to enjoy being newlyweds for a while. Although anyone who knows them, knows their relationship is solid. The bond they share is tight, and I cannot think of two people more deserving or who would be better parents. I think back to Liam and how he was before falling in love with Allison. It's hard to picture that guy as a dad, but this Liam, the one that is madly in love with his wife, yeah, I can see it. Their kids are going to be smothered with love.

Liam grins at me. "Yep, Auntie Hales."

"Do Mom and Dad know?" I ask them.

Allison bumps her should with Liam's. "No, we haven't really discussed telling anyone we were even trying. It could take a while and they say you shouldn't tell anyone until you are past your first trimester," Allison explains.

"Mom and Dad are going to go freaking crazy," I say because it's true. My parents are going to be the best grandparents ever. That kid will never want for anything.

Liam throws his arm over Allie's shoulder and pulls her into his chest, placing a kiss to her temple. "We're going to wait to tell them until we know for sure and Allie feels like it's been enough time. We can't keep this from the two of you," he says.

Allison reaches her hand across the table and lays it on top of mind. "I'm going to need my sister through this," she says almost in question.

Is she serious right now? Hell yeah, I am so there. "I'm here for whatever you need. And, of course, if it's a girl, I expect her name to be Hailey," I say to lighten the mood. The four of us erupt in laughter.

"Hales, I'm not even pregnant." She shrugs. "Who knows how long it will take."

Liam breaks out in a huge grin. "Practice makes perfect, baby." He wags his eyebrows for added theatrics. My brother is a goofy ass when it comes to Allison.

We continue to laugh and joke as Allie and I finish our meal. The guys finished long before we did. I help Allison and the guys retreat to the living room, talking football.

"I really am happy for you, Allie," I say to my best friend and sister. I will always be thankful that Allie and I were paired to room together freshman year. Even more so, I will be forever grateful to Gran for pushing Allie to go away to college. What is it she used to say? Something about life being a canvas and painting your way. Allie has a canvas print with the saying hanging on their bedroom wall. Liam had it made for her.

Allison is quiet, not saying a word. I finish adding soap to the dishwasher and turn to face her. She is sitting on top of the kitchen counter with tears running down her face. I drop the hand towel and rush to her side. My mind races with what has got her so upset. If Liam did anything...

"Allie, what's wrong?" I ask, standing in front of her. I reach over and grab a napkin and hand it to her.

She shakes her head no. I can see a faint smile form on her lips. At this point, I'm not sure if the tears are happy or sad. She wipes her eyes and clears her throat. "Hales, my heart is so full. So full it aches." I watch as her trembling hand tries to keep up with the tears that fall from her eyes.

Before I can comment, the guys come busting into the room. They both carry what appear to be empty beer bottles. Liam stops in his tracks when he sees Allie in tears. He thrusts his bottle toward Aiden, who thank goodness has excellent reflexes, and he gently but eagerly pushes me out of the way and replaces me. He steps in between Allie's legs and his big hands hold her face. Her bends down so they are eye level. "Talk to me, beautiful; why the tears?" he asks as he tries to wipe them away with his thumbs.

Allison frames Liam's face mirroring him. "These are happy tears. It's a little overwhelming to have your dreams come true. It was just Gran and me for so long and now I'm married to this amazing man, who wants to make babies with me." She kisses his nose. "My heart is full," she whispers.

I feel Aiden come up behind me and wrap his arms around my waist. He rests his chin on my shoulder. "She deserves this," he whispers in my ear.

"More than anyone," I whisper back and I settle against him.

"Maybe we should practice making babies," Aiden says, nipping my earlobe.

I turn in his arms and place both hands behind his neck. Lifting up on tiptoes I whisper in his ear. "Liam did say practice makes perfect."

Aiden growls as his lips capture mine. "Thanks for dinner, Allie We gotta jet," he yells over his shoulder. Without another word, he turns and heads for the door. I hear Allison and Liam laughing at us.

"Call me," Allison replies. I wave at her and offer her a sheepish grin as my fiancé carries me out the door.

Chapter Thirteen

L iam

Today my little sister marries my best friend. I can honestly say I never thought those words would come out of my mouth, but I cannot be happier for both of them. Aiden once told me that Hailey was his Allison. That's all it took for me to understand the love he has for her. Who am I to keep my little sister from something so surreal? Not many people find this type of love in their lifetime and I'm glad that both my little sis and I have it.

It was not even a month ago that Allison and I were promising till death do us part. That was the night Aiden proposed to Hailey. They both agreed that waiting was not an option for them. Fuck, if I could have gotten Allison to marry me the day I proposed, I would have been all over it. Instead, I let my beautiful girl plan her dream wedding. My only stipulation was it had to be within a year. I didn't have the patience to wait any longer than that.

I feel my wife. She must have finished helping Hailey get dressed. Yes, I said I feel her. Our souls are so deeply entwined that I know when she walks into a room. I stopped trying to figure it out a long time ago; I just roll with it. She has the same uncanny abilities when it comes to me.

Her hands sneak around my waist. "Penny for your thoughts?" she asks.

I place my hands over the top of hers and lace our fingers together. "Just thinking about our wedding day. How you made me the happiest man alive," I tell her. I watch as her eyes go soft at my admission.

"Ditto," she says, resting her cheek against my back.

Tugging on our joined hands, I guide her to stand in front of me. I wrap my arms around her waist and bury my face in her neck. I will thank my lucky stars every day for the rest of my life that she gave me a chance.

"Today has been a long time coming."

"Yes, it has. Those two have fought tooth and nail to get where they are today."

"Knock, knock," my mom says as she walks into our suite.

"Mom, we are newlyweds you know. You could have walked in while we were in a compromising position." I pretend to be appalled.

She waves her hand in the air to let me know she wasn't worried. "Good, that means I'm one step closer to grandbabies," she retorts.

I feel Allison stiffen in my arms and I squeez her tighter. I bend to whisper in her ear. "Relax, she has no idea. She just wants grandkids," I say, kissing her cheek.

"At least I have double the chance after today," Mom continues to talk about wanting to be a grandma.

"What do you have double the chance of?" Dad walks in holding four bottles of water, passing them out to each of us.

"Being a grandma," Mom tells him.

Dad slaps his hands together with glee. He turns to face us. "Yes. Please tell me you're working on it."

I look down and watch as Allison's face goes beet read. "Dad." I scold him. Really, I couldn't care less. Were married, and even if we weren't, I wouldn't care. I love her. End of story.

Dad grins. "Hey, you can't blame us for trying. We want to be grandparents while we're still in our prime. I don't want to be walking with a cane trying to teach him or her or both," he winks at Allison, "to try and play catch."

"Yes, we want to be the cool, hip grandparents," Mom joins in.

I cannot help but laugh and the craziness that is my parents.

Mom comes over and pulls on Allie's hand, taking her away from me. "Hey." I protest.

"Shush you. We have to go to Hales. You two need to head over and see if Aiden needs any final words of wisdom," she scolds.

Dad and I look at each other then back to Mom and Allison. "Love her," we say in unison.

The girls smile and wave as they walk out the door.

iden

I'm pacing the floor and I keep checking my watch. Twenty more minutes until she's mine. Officially mine. Fuck, this has been a long time coming. I have loved that girl for years. We've fought hard for this and now it's all coming together.

"Son, you're going to wear a hole in the carpet," my dad chuckles from the couch.

"Time has stopped," I say, checking my watch yet again.

Dad roars with laughter and that's how Liam and my future father-in-law find us.

"What's so funny?" Mr. MacCoy asks Dad.

Dad motions his head toward me. "My son is about to wear a hole in the carpet. He seems to think time has stopped," he explains his laughter.

"Dude, don't I fucking know it. I thought the wait for Allison to walk down that aisle was going to kill me," Liam sympathizes.

Mr. MacCoy walks to me and places his hand on my shoulder in a firm grip. I don't give him the chance to speak before my mouth opens and, "I just fucking love her so much. I've waited a long damn time for this," spills out.

A huge smile crosses his face. "I know you do. I wouldn't willing give my baby girl to just anyone. Be good to each other," he says, his grip still firm on my shoulder.

Mr. and Mrs. MacCoy are amazing people, so much like my own parents that they have become close friends the four of them. He knows me. He knows what she means to me, but I can still see the sadness in his eyes mixed in with happiness for both of us.

I reach out and wrap him in a hug. "You loved her first, I know that. I will love her until my last breath," I say for his ears only.

I see the slight nod of his head that he heard me. With one last pat on the back, we break apart.

Liam looks up from his phone. "My beautiful wife has just informed me that it's time for us to take our places on the beach."

I nod in agreement and they follow me out of the suite. My girl wants to get married at sunset and that's exactly what she's getting. We don't want frill; we just want to be married. We met earlier today with the ordained minister that the resort keeps on the payroll. We advised him that we want this quick. No strung out vows, quick and to the point. We just want to be married.

Harbour Island is beautiful, but the sunset in Harbour Island is breathtaking. My girl knew what she was doing when she booked this place. I look out over the ocean at the setting sun and take deep, soothing breaths. I'm waiting for Hailey and her dad to walk toward me. Within minutes I will be a married man. Hell fucking yes.

Again, trying to control my breathing, I feel a tap on my shoulder. I turn to look and almost stop breathing. Hailey, on her dad's arm, is walking toward me in a white strapless dress. The dress cups her breasts and fits firm around her belly. Then it flows out in what looks like such soft fabric as it blows with the ocean breeze as it drags against the sand. I'm not into fashion, but the dress, which could have come from fucking Walmart for all I care, looks amazing on her. She truly looks like an angel walking toward me at sunset.

I feel my hand start to tremble as she gets closer. I'm not nervous, hell no. I want this; I want her. The tremble is from the excitement running through my veins. We fought the battle and we won. I have waited so long for this moment and it's here.

Hailey steps next to me, her dad in between us. I hear the minister asks who gives her to me. I can hear voices, and I know from last night's rehearsal that Mr. MacCoy is saying the he and Mrs. MacCoy do. However, the words are muffled. My eyes are locked on hers and she is all I see. She is all I will ever want, need. My angel.

I feel strong hands clasp mine and I am forced to remove my eyes from my bride. My father-in-law has his hands clasped over both mine and Hailey's. The minister says something that doesn't register as Mr. MacCoy tells me to take care of his little girl.

"Till my last breath," I whisper. I know he hears me from the nod of his head. He kisses Hales on the cheek and then goes to stand by his wife.

My eyes find hers again, my Hales, my wife. Could life possibly get any better than this?

Hailey reaches for my other hand and her eyes widen. "You're trembling," she says, her voice soft, just for me.

I nod yes and swallow hard. I'm about to lose my shit. I'm glad we chose an intimate gathering. "You're not nervous?"

"No. You make me brave, Aiden. Standing here with you is my dream come true."

"I've wanted this day for so long." My voice cracks with emotion and I feel a tear slide down my cheek.

Hailey nods at the minister, telling him to get the show on the road. I repeat when I am supposed to. Hailey guides me by squeezing my hands to alert me that it's my turn to speak. She's so beautiful; I can't take my eyes off her. It's not until I hear the words, "You may kiss your bride," that I finally break free of the hold she has on me and kiss her with everything I have in me.

"I love you, Hailey Emerson," I whisper against her lips as I dive back in for another kiss.

Hailey giggles as she pulls away and says, "I think I'm going to enjoy being Mrs. Emerson."

Chapter Fifteen

A llison

The wedding is simple perfection, just what Hales wanted. I'm watching as Aiden goes in for yet another kiss while we all whoop and holler at the newlyweds. Finally, he releases her and the parents move in to give their congratulations. Liam slides in behind me and wraps me in his arms. His lips immediately find my neck as he peppers me with warm, wet kisses.

"I love you, Mrs. MacCoy," he whispers in my ear. The feel of his hot breath along with his sweet words have my body tingling. Every single time he touches me I feel it. My body is so in tune with him.

I turn so we are now face to face, chest to chest. I place both of my hands behind his neck and begin to run my fingers through his hair. Looking up, my eyes lock with his. "I love you too." I barely get the words out before his lips are on mine. I don't hesitate to open for him. His tongue traces my bottom lip before sliding next to mine. Liam releases a growl and pulls me tightly against him. This is how they find us.

"Hey, you had your turn, big brother. This is my day," Hales jokes.

Liam pulls back and rests his forehead against mine. "Have you seen my wife?" he retorts.

Everyone laughs good-naturedly and I feel my face flush crimson. Liam traces his index finger across my cheek. "You're beautiful," he says softly.

"We're surrounded by newlyweds," I hear Mr. MacCoy say.

I turn my head and see that Hailey and Aiden are in a similar stance as Liam and I. I giggle, which catches everyone's attention. Before long, we are all in a fit of laughter.

"Let's eat so I can start my wedding night," Aiden says as he lifts Hailey in his arms and carries her to the private dining room that we reserved for dinner.

The private dining room is amazing. Soft lighting surrounds a large round table so the eight of us can sit and enjoy each other's company. We have two waiters and they are efficient as ever. They don't linger and slip in and out almost unnoticed. Of course, this is a high-end resort.

The food is amazing, as is the company. It's nice how the eight of us are all together. Two couples beginning their journey of life and love, and two who are entering yet another phase. A phase where all four of them would enjoy grandchildren to be a part of. They have mentioned it several times during dinner; how we could take family vacations and they could spoil the grandkids with summer trips to Disney.

Liam just smiles and rolls his eyes as he leans over with one hand behind my chair and the other resting on my belly. He whispers in my ear, "We better amp up our practice regimen. I would hate to disappoint them." He sits back in his chair with a smirk on his face.

Two can play that game. I tug on his shirt sleeve and motion for him to come closer. He bends his head so he can hear me. "What if we already made a baby? We will no longer need to practice," I say smugly as I sit back in my chair. I act all badass at my confession, but really I'm freaking out. I should get my period any day now. I haven't mentioned it to Liam. He would have me peeing on sticks hourly. I know these things take time, so I'm not getting my hopes up.

Keeping his head down, he turns so his lips meet my ear. "We'll need to keep our skills up for the next one." He nips at my earlobe and I bite my bottom lip to keep from moaning and embarrassing myself yet again in front of our family.

I thank my lucky stars each and every day that the Emersons lived next door to Gran. My friendship with Aiden led me to Hailey and Liam. Their parents, just like the Emersons, have welcomed me with open arms. I never dreamed the day I left for college that my journey would lead me here. I miss Gran and my parents every day, but the love I have found sitting around this table fills me with so much joy. My hand automatically rests on my stomach. Soon Liam and I will have our own little family. Tears spring to my eyes at just the thought. I can't wait to be a mom.

Liam leans over and places his large hand over mine. "What's wrong?" he asks. I can hear the concern in his voice, see it in his eyes.

"Nothing," I croak out.

"Why the tears, baby?" he asks, tucking my hair behind my ear with his other hand.

"These are happy tears. I'm so blessed to be a part of all of this." I motion around the table. It's then that I realize all eyes are on me. I decide to just lay it out there. Taking a deep breath, I say, "I love every single one of you so much. I've always wanted a big family; you have all made my dreams come true." I place my hand on Liam's cheek. "You're my dream come true," I say softly, my eyes never leaving his.

"You're everything, beautiful girl," he says, pulling me into his lap and holding me close.

Chapter Sixteen

H ailey

Aiden hasn't stopped touching me since we met at the altar. His hand on the small of my back, resting on my thigh, arm around my shoulder, lips against every part of my skin he can get away with in front of our families. He's driving me crazy.

I love our families. I love how they flew all the way here to share this moment with us, on short notice no less. However, right now, all I want to do is escape to our private overwater bungalow and lose myself in my husband. I need reassurance that this isn't just a dream, that Aiden and I really are married. As if he can read my mind, Aiden brings his lips to my ear.

"I love you, Mrs. Emerson," he breathes. Goose bumps break out across my skin. Hailey Emerson, that's me. This is real and I can't wait any longer.

I gently scoot back in my chair and stand. Without missing a beat, Aiden stands with me. His arm immediately goes around my waist and we step behind our chairs. "Thank you all so much for being here, being a part of this." I look up at Aiden. "I just need a minute with my husband," I say softly. I know our family heard what I said. I wasn't trying to prevent it. However, I only have eyes for Aiden.

Without another word, he leads me out of our private dining room. I hear laughter and words of congratulations and finally their happily ever after, but we don't stop to respond. Another advantage of a small intimate wedding is that you don't have to spend hours making rounds and thanking those who came to wish you well. You don't have to spend hours waiting to be one with your new husband. Best idea ever.

Aiden keeps one arm firmly around my waist as he leads us to our bungalow. Aiden opens the door, placing his hand on the small of my back and guiding me inside. I walk toward the bed but stop when I feel his hand at my elbow.

"Dance with me, angel." His voice is gruff with desire.

"There's no music," I say. Not that we need music. Aiden and I can make our own music.

He reaches into the pocket of his cargo shorts and pulls out his phone. He swipes the screen and I hear Blake Shelton's "My Eyes" fill the room. He tosses his phone on the bed as he leads me to the center of the room. We're standing on top of the glass floor. The water is so iridescent that it glows in the moonlight, the rays softly lighting the room. It's the most romantic thing I've ever seen, well almost. Nothing will beat the view Aiden created the night he proposed to me.

He wraps his arms around me and pulls me close. I wrap my hands around the nape of his neck. He gently lifts my chin so we are eye to eye. The song he chose is fitting for the moment. Leave it to Aiden to be able to find a song that fits us perfectly on the fly.

As the song comes to an end, Aiden leans into me and I instantly come on my tiptoes to meet him halfway. Our lips meet in a slow sensual dance. We take our time tasting each other. Our tongues gently glide with the other as our hands roam each other's body.

Aiden pulls back and rests his forehead against mine. "I want to make love to you, Mrs. Emerson," he whispers.

I don't respond; there are no words even if I wanted to. I can't explain how it feels to know that he's mine. That we are married and can be together. Live happily ever after. I turn so my back is to him. He gathers up my hair and places it over my shoulder. I feel his hands and they gently caress my shoulders before he finds my zipper. I feel the release of the material as Aiden releases the zipper. He gently runs his index finger up and down my spine.

I turn to face him with only my hands holding my dress to my chest. Aiden's eyes are so full of love and want. He reaches for my left hand and laces our fingers together. He does the same with the right. My dress falls to the floor. I watch him as he takes in the sight of me. His eyes roam over every inch of my body. My dress was so fitted at the top with a built-in corset that a bra was not necessary. I'm standing before my new husband in nothing but a white lace thong.

He drops to his knees and laces both hands on my hips. I watch every move he makes. I want to remember this night. His eyes find mine. "Baby, you take my breath away," he says, peppering kisses against my thighs. His hands move lower as he hooks a finger into each side of my thong. He slowly removes it, stopping to place gentle kisses on each leg. Once I feel the material around my ankles, I lift one leg then the other to remove them.

Aiden stands to his full height and picks me up, cradling me in his arms. He gently lays me on the bed. He makes quick work of stripping out of his clothes before crawling over top of me. "This is our forever, baby," he says as he settles himself between my legs.

He reaches to the nightstand. I know what he's reaching for. I have yet to get on birth control. Nursing school and clinicals were so hectic I just never took the time to go. Aiden always says it's my body and my choice. Tonight, on our wedding night, I don't want anything between us. This is something that we have talked about how it would feel. Aiden is the only guy I've ever been with and he has never not used a condom. Tonight I want all of him; I want all of my husband.

I reach for his arm and tug. "No," I say softly. His eyes snap to mine. I can see him trying to process what I'm saying. "I don't want anything between us. I want to feel you, all of you," I confess.

Aiden leans in for a kiss. "Baby, are you sure? We've never..." He swallows hard. "I've never...God, I want that. I want to feel you," he says breathlessly.

I lift my hips. "Make love to me, husband." I don't stop to think about the consequences. I just want to feel him, all of him.

Chapter Seventeen

L iam

It's definitely not a hardship as a newlywed to be in paradise with my wife. Tonight after Aiden and Hales left, our parents decided to go visit one of the clubs. Allie and I declined; instead, deciding to take a moonlit stroll on the beach. Allie has been stressed the last couple of days. She is due to start her cycle any time. She thinks I don't know, but how could I not. She's my wife, my world. I make it my business to know everything about her. I know how her mood changes, she goes through at least one tub of butter pecan ice cream, and showers are at least twice a day during.

I really just want to hand her one of the many tests I bought, just to see. The test guarantees early detection, seven days before others. I ordered a case of them at the local pharmacy. I've read how these things take time and how we can potentially go through a lot of tests. Besides, I want lots of babies with her. We'll use them eventually. I even packed a few in our luggage. I was sure she would find them, but her mind has been so preoccupied since we got here.

As we stroll down the beach, I watch as Allison yawns, again. She has been doing that a lot the last few days. I hate how she's stressing herself out over this. I know how bad she wants to be a mom, but if she is pregnant, this isn't good for the baby. I lead us toward a lounger and sit down, pulling her into my lap. She leans in for a kiss and suddenly doesn't seem as tired. I situate us so I can slip my hand underneath her sundress without it being obvious. Hales said this resort is known for its privacy for celebrities, but you never can be too safe. I inch my hand up her dress.I trace the outer edge of her thong and she hums her approval into my mouth. I have to keep my hand moving, or this can get out of control and fast. I don't want that happening out here. I tend to lose myself in her and I don't want to take the chance of getting caught by the paparazzi.

My hand traces up her ribcage and she sucks in a breath at the contact. I smile against her lips, kissing her again. Once I reach her breast, I gently caress her and she yelps as if she's in pain. I stop and watch her eyes. "Sorry, I just...they're just tender. I think you've worked me over too much with this baby making business," she says with a soft smile.

My thoughts immediately jump to the book I was reading on the plane. Allison slept most of the flight. I pulled out my iPad and dove into one of those pregnancy books. What to expect or something, I can't remember exactly. I overheard one of the guys on the team talking about how he was reading it. He said it helps explain what his wife was going through. The early sign of pregnancy is tender breasts, and now that I think of it, being tired was also mentioned. She hasn't mentioned anything about being nauseous, but maybe she will get lucky and skip that part.

I guide her head to my chest and gently stroke her hair. Her hair feels like silk and I love to run my fingers through it. My heart is pounding because I know with everything in me that my wife is pregnant. I just have this feeling. I take a few deep breaths trying to calm my excitement. I need to get her back to the room and talk her into taking a test. I hate the thought of crushing her if the test is negative, but my gut tells me that will not be the case.

We sit there a little longer, and I try to focus on taking slow, even breaths. The excitement building inside of me that I'm going to be a father is overwhelming. I need to get her back to the suite. "Ready to call it a night, beautiful girl?" I ask her.

Sitting up with a yawn, she answers, "Yes, I'm exhausted."

I can't help but grin at her. "What's that look for?" she asks.

"Nothing, baby, just ready to get you in our bed," I say, winking at her. I have no idea how I am going to bring up the test idea.

Once we are back in our suite, we strip down and head to the shower. The shower stall is massive just like the one we have at home. I sit down on the bench and she straddles my hips. We make love under the rainfall shower head. I have got to get one of these in our shower at home. After a quick wash, I slip out and allow Allie to finish washing her hair. I quickly dry off and slip on a pair of boxer briefs. I place one of the pregnancy tests that I brought with me on the counter. I had it hidden under my towel.

I lean back against the counter, arms crossed over my chest and legs crossed at the ankles. Allies steps out and I drink in the sight of her. I watch as she wrings the water out of her hair and wipes the remaining drops from her skin. She smiles at me, knowing I can't take my eyes off of her anytime she is near. She walks to the other side of the double sink to brush her teeth, just as I knew she would. I turn and begin to brush mine as well. I watch her closely in the mirror, waiting for her to notice the test.

She bends down to rinse out her mouth and her eyes widen. She looks in the mirror, knowing I'm still watching her. I watch her as she finishes, wipes her mouth on a hand towel, and places her toothbrush in the holder. "Liam?" she asks. Her voice is filled with confusion and excitement.

"Baby, I know it's close to time. I've been reading this book—"

"What book?" she interjects.

I shrug. "I can't remember the name. It's a book about pregnancy and what to expect. One of the guys on the team was saying how it helped him when his girl was pregnant. I brought it on the flight over while you slept and read the first several chapters," I explain.

"Where did the test come from?" she questions.

"Well...I kind of ordered a case of them. I know these things take time, and I just figured we would go through them."

She watches me, then stares at the test. She brings her eyes back to me. She doesn't say anything just stares at the box. "Allie," I say, reaching for her. "Baby, I have this feeling, I think we're pregnant. Can you take the test?" I ask her.

It seems like eternity before she raises her eyes back to mine. "What if I'm not? What it it's too early?"

"Baby, this test is for early detection. If we're not, we keep trying. I don't mind, do you?" I wink at her, trying to lighten the mood to calm her fears. "Allie, I have this gut feeling that we are going to get the results we want. Please. I'm right here, beautiful. We do this together, you and me," I say as I pull her into my arms and kiss the top of her head.

Chapter Eighteen

iden

Hailey bucks her hips into mine and I have to raise up on my arms to prevent from sliding into her. I need a minute. This is a first for me. It's fitting that I share this with my wife. God, this beautiful angel is mine.

"Hales, are you sure? This is not something we have to do," I tell her. I know that we're married now, but damn it, I need for her to be sure that this is a risk she's willing to take. Even if I pull out, there's a chance of her getting pregnant.

"Yes," she says, her voice breathy. "I want you. I want to feel all of you inside of me."

I lower myself back between her legs, my eyes never leaving hers. "I love you, Hales," I say as I slide inside of her, bare. I slide inside as far as I can go and still. I need a minute. Hales moans and wiggles her hips.

"Aiden."

"Baby, I need a minute. I just...Holy fuck, you feel amazing. I've never felt anything like it. So soft and warm. I just...need a minute," I say, closing my eyes to get myself under control. This is the most amazing thing I have ever felt in my entire life. One thrust into her with no barrier and I'm ready to come. In fact, I almost did. Some wedding night that would have been.

Hailey giggles. Giggles. "You little vixen," I say with nothing but love behind the words. I rock my hips into her and her giggles turn into moans. I try like hell to take it slow, to make this moment last. The first time ever making love to my wife, my Hales. The louder she moans, the faster I pump into her. "Baby, I'm close," I say against her neck. I ease up ready to pull out of her when she locks her legs around my back.

"Angel?" I question as I continue to move in and out of her, trying like hell not to combust.

"Don't pull out," she moans. "I want all of you, Aiden. Every last drop."

It's with her words that I let go and spill over inside of her. She follows me over the edge. I can't help but relax against her, still inside of her. I try to hold my weight on my arms, but I'm wiped. That was the single most intense orgasm of my life.

I lean up to pull out of her and she tightens her legs back around my waist. "Don't, not yet," she pleads.

I softly kiss her lips. "I don't want to crush you," I explain.

"You're not. I just need you where you are. Inside of me. Please."

What kind of husband would I be to deny my wife what she wants on our wedding night? I gently rest my weight against her and bury my face in her neck, breathing her in. I will remember this moment for as long as I live.

We lay there for what seems like eternity. Once our breathing slows, I gently pull out of her, immediately missing her heat. I roll on my side and pull her back against my chest. "I love you so fucking much, Hailey. I never thought we would get here. I will never forget tonight, you, this moment. Our first time as husband and wife." I kiss her shoulder.

She rolls over so we are face to face. She runs her fingers through my shaggy hair. I offered to get it cut for the wedding, but she threated bodily harm. "Tonight was magical. Not just this," she points her finger at her chest and then mine, "but the entire wedding. It was perfect. Just as I imagined." She snuggles in closer, placing a soft kiss on my chest. "Making love to you, with nothing between us, it was unlike anything we've ever shared. It was like you were a part of me."

I hug her tight, not willing to let her go for a minute. I need her as close to me as possible. "Trust me, baby. I felt you. You're soft and warm. The feeling of you around me is so fucking tight when you come. I never realized how a condom made that much of a difference."

She smiles at me. "Maybe it's just us. Mr. and Mrs. Aiden Emerson. Maybe that's just how married life is going to be for us," she says.

"God, angel, I sure the hell hope so. Nothing can compete with the feeling of being inside you like that. Nothing."

She makes a noise that I think means she agrees as she settles against my chest. I keep my arms wrapped tightly around her as we drift off to sleep.

Chapter Nineteen

llison

I pull out of Liam's embrace and reach for the box on the counter. I read over the packaging. Sure enough, it says the test is made for early detection up to seven days before a missed period. I'm due to start any day now. I think about what Liam said about reading his book. I can't help but smile at my husband. He's the most amazing man and I want this with him, more than anything.

Liam explained the book he is reading said that being tired and sensitive breasts were signs of pregnancy. I have been exhausted this last week, but I blamed it on packing and the long flight. This last month has been crazy for us. I noticed a few nights ago that my breasts were tender. That also happens when you are getting ready to start your period, so I didn't really think much of it. Tonight, when Liam was touching me, they were more than tender. That's never happened before. I flip the box over, reading the rest of the packaging. Apparently, there will be a plus sign for positive and a negative sign for negative. It's digital read out. I'm sure Liam bought the most expensive one, and he said he bought an entire case.

Taking a deep breath, I open one end of the box. I pull open the tabs and pull out the test. It's wrapped in more packaging. I hand Liam the box with the instructions still inside. The outside of the box says results in five minutes. Reading the result is easy with a positive or negative sign and peeing on the stick is not rocket science. I tear open the packing that is holding the test and pull off the cap. I walk toward the toilet. Liam turns and I grab his arm. "Stay," I say.

He leans down to kiss my forehead. "I'm just going to go get my phone for the timer."

I nod in agreement and watch as he walks out the door. I stand there by the toilet with the test in my hand. This little stick could change our lives. Liam said he has a gut feeling that we're pregnant. I love how he says "we're," not me. Us. He's all in with starting a family and I couldn't be happier. I don't know what I did to deserve a man like Liam. Liam says I changed him, but he changed me too. We make each other better.

Liam comes rushing back into the room; he was gone maybe thirty seconds. He holds up his phone where his stopwatch app is already opened. He's wearing a huge grin across his face. "Let's do this," I say as I sit on the toilet and start the awkwardness that is peeing on a stick with your husband watching. Who can pee on command with an audience?

"Allie, I can step out," he tells me.

"No. You said we are in this together. I need you here," I tell him. I can't explain it, but I just need him here. I don't want to do this alone. I know he could come back in as soon as I am done, but I just…want him to be a part of all of it. Him and me against the world.

Finally, I'm able to do my business. Liam hands me the cap and I place it back on the end of the stick, lying it flat on the bathroom counter. I wash my hands and wait. Liam sits his phone on the counter beside the pregnancy test and pulls me into his arms. I feel him kiss the top of my head. We don't speak, we just hold each other and wait.

The buzz of the timer startles me. Liam reaches for his phone, while his eyes stay glued to mine. He swipes at the screen to turn off the timer. He places the phone back on the counter, never breaking eye contact. "Are you ready, baby?" he asks, cupping my cheeks.

"As I'll ever be," I reply.

Liam turns me so I am facing the counter as he wraps his arms around me from behind. My eyes are closed. I feel his arm reach around for the stick. He sucks in a deep breath, releasing it slowly. My eyes are still closed. I'm waiting for him to tell me. "Open your eyes, baby." His voice low.

I slowly open my eyes and I see Liam with his hand in the air holding the pregnancy test. I follow his muscled arm to his hand. I love his hands. That's when I see it. The plus sign. Holy shit. We're having a baby.

I turn to face him and jump into his arms. He catches me with ease, holding me tight against him. "We're having a baby, beautiful girl," he whispers in my ear.

I'm sobbing tears against his naked chest. He just holds me. I feel us moving and assume Liam is taking us to bed. Once we are out of the bathroom, he starts spinning us in circles and yells, "hell yeah." at the top of his lungs.

I laugh through my tears at his celebration. When we finally stop spinning, he lays me down gently on the bed.

"Precious cargo," he says, his hand resting on my belly. "I love you so much, Allison MacCoy."

More tears spring to my eyes. I'm not really sure they ever stopped. "I love you too." I fight to get the words out through my tears. This is really happening. Liam and I are going to be parents. I take a deep breath to control my tears. "Thank you for making my dreams come true." With that, I pull him on top of me and kiss him until we are breathless.

Chapter Twenty

H ailey

I groan as I hear Aiden's alarm clock blaring from his side of the bed and throw the covers over my head to help drown out the sound. I hear my husband chuckle beside me. Our flight home from the Bahamas was delayed and we didn't get in until after midnight. It's freaking five in the damn morning. "What are you doing?" I mumble through my sleep filled haze.

"I need to hit the gym," he says, his voice low.

"Why the hell are you whispering? I'm already awake," I question.

Aiding laughs louder this time. "Go back to sleep, wife of mine. I'm staying and working at the home gym today. I'll bring you breakfast in a few hours." He places a soft, yet wet, kiss on my cheek and jumps off the bed.

"Uh," I groan as I wipe my cheek with the blanket. Damn chipper man and his morning workouts. He refuses to miss a day, even if it's the off season. He and Liam met up at the villa's gym while we were on our honeymoon. I can't blame him, the League is a vicious company to be a part of. You need to stay on top of your game or be replaced. Aiden and Liam have busted their asses to get where they are and both strive every day to get better.

Today, I want to sleep in and finish unpacking all of my boxes from the condo. Aiden convinced me not to rush to find a nursing position. He thinks we should settle in first. There are still several rooms in the house that are sparsely furnished. Aiden insisted I be a part of that. On the weekends I did have free from nursing school, we didn't want to waste our time buying furniture. So, we plan to finish decorating the house in the next few weeks as well. I drift off to sleep thinking about what needs to be done.

A few hours later, the sun is shining through the windows and I feel the bed slightly dip. I peel open one eye to find Aiden holding a bowl of my favorite breakfast, vanilla yogurt with granola and fresh strawberries and a bottle of water.

"Good morning, Mrs.Emerson." He settles in beside me.

"Good morning, Mr. Emerson." I offer him a cheeky smile.

Aiden hands me my breakfast and I dig in. "How was your workout?" I ask before shoveling in another bite.

"Good. Liam called and wants to know if we want to get together tonight for a cookout. I told him they could come here, that it was our turn to host."

"Sounds good, anything particular you have in mind?"

"Nope, thought I might fire up the grill. Liam and I can freeze our asses off grilling some burgers while you ladies sit inside and talk about how amazing your husbands are," he retorts, the smile never leaving his face.

"And what makes you think we will be talking about how amazing you are? Maybe we have wifely things to bitch about. We need to use our girl time wisely," I fire back at him.

Aiden throws his head back in laughter. "I told them six o'clock. We need to stock up on groceries. I ran to the store and picked up a few things for breakfast, but the kitchen is bare."

"Anything else on the agenda for today?" I ask, taking my last bite of yogurt.

"Not really. I know you wanted to try and get everything unpacked and stowed away. I'm at your service. You just tell me what you need and where you need it and I'm your man."

"Oh, honey, look at you. You are taking on the role of husband with grace. You already understand that I will be wearing the pants and assigning the honey do list," I say, trying like hell not to bust up laughing.

"That's fine with me as long as I get to call the shots when the day is done. I still have so many things I need to do with you as my wife," he tells me.

"I just need to hop in the shower," I tell him.

I'm sitting on my knees and start to crawl to the end of the bed to climb out, but Aiden grabs me and thrusts his hips into my rear. "Like this. I've never had my wife like this," he informs me, his voice husky with desire.

I'm only wearing a thong, so I wiggle my barely covered ass against his erection, which is clearly not hidden in his basketball shorts. I hear Aiden growl, and the next thing I know, my throng is removed from my body and my husband is rocking into me.

Needless to say, my shower is delayed.

Chapter Twenty-One

L iam

I called Aiden while Allison was sleeping, right after my workout, to invite them over for dinner. Allie and I are dying to give them our news. We aren't ready to tell my parents just yet. The only reason we are telling Aiden and Hales is because they know we are trying, or were trying since we are. Well, and the fact that we want to shout it from the fucking rooftops, but we know we should wait until after she is through her first trimester. I am so fucking stoked about being a dad. My dad was amazing, both of my parents are amazing.

Allison is glowing with excitement and I cannot wait to watch as her body changes. I can barely keep my hands off her now; I can only imagine how bad it's going to be when it's obvious that my baby is growing inside of her. I read that pregnancy book on the flight home. It said some women have an increased sex drive during pregnancy. Hell fucking yes. My wife is always up for some loving, but I, as her husband, will make sure I fulfill my duty of giving into her every whim while she's pregnant. Hell, who am I kidding? I do that now. I just can't say no to her; it's not possible.

I head back upstairs to take a quick shower and, if she's still asleep, climb in bed with my wife. Just as I make it to the top of the steps, I hear, "Damn it, Liam." I rush into our room to find out what happened.

"Allie, baby, are you okay?" I call out to her as I follow her muffled curse to the bathroom. The door is slightly ajar, so I push through and what I see has my dick going hard in an instant. I start toward her, but stop when she snaps her head up and glares at me. What the hell?

"Don't do it, MacCoy," she warns me. Allison reaches in and turns on the shower.

"What's wrong, baby? I heard you scream; I was worried," I tell her. I inch toward her even though she continues to glare at me.

"What's wrong? I'll tell you what's wrong. You left the damn toilet seat up again. I sat down to pee and ended up in the damn bowl." she yells at me, finger pointing and all.

I try really hard not to laugh, because the thought of her falling in the toilet is priceless. I fail miserably as the scene runs through my mind and burst out laughing. This causes a death glare from my wife. "Baby, come on. That's funny and you know it," I say through my laughter.

"Kiss my ass, Liam. That shit is not funny. How would you like your ass bathed in toilet water first thing in the morning? All you have to do is drop the damn seat once you are done. Is that too much to ask?" she seethes.

Fuck me. She's really pissed. This is not the first time this has happened. It is, however, the first time I have been home when it did. My laughter dies when I see how angry she really is. I watch as she steps into the hot spray. I stand and watch her. This woman is my world and she's carrying my baby. I need to be more sensitive to her needs. Allison doesn't ask me for anything, well, except to put the damn toilet seat down. I need to make an effort to re-train myself.

I watch as she lathers up her hair. She turns to rinse and I follow the shampoo as it cascades down her body. I pull my shirt over my head and drop my gym shorts to the floor. I pull open the shower door and step in behind her.

"You could have waited until I was done," she scolds me. She continues with her shower as if I'm not standing right in front of her. As she turns so her back is facing me, I make my move.

I grab her hips and bring her back against my chest. I feel her shudder at the contact. Leaning down, I bury my face in her neck and trace circles with my tongue. I make my way up to her ear. "I'm sorry, beautiful. I'll do better, I promise." My lips glide back down her neck as I work my way toward her collarbone. I nip and lick until I feel her relax against me. Reaching around, I trace my fingers through her folds and she's wet, just like I knew she would be.

"Liam," she moans.

My name from her lips in that sexy voice, I know I'm forgiven. "Brace your hands on the wall, baby," I whisper against her ear. She does what I say. I know she's ready for me, so there is no need for further delay. I gently guide myself into her heat. I'm reminded again that this girl was made for me. Every single fucking time I'm inside of her, it feels better than the last.

"I need more," she says, wiggling her hips and pushing back against me.

"Tell me, beautiful," I say as I slow down my strokes. I know what she wants, but I love to hear her say it. To have my beautiful wife begging me to fuck her, yeah nothing better.

"Harder. Please, Liam." She moans as I increase my speed. She meets me thrust for thrust and I lose control, unleashing on her. "Liam, I'm...ahhh."

She screams and I can feel her clench around me. A few more deep strokes and I'm falling over the edge with her. Leaning down, I place a kiss on her back just below her shoulder.

I grab her loofa and body wash and begin washing her. She returns the favor, neither one of us talking about the earlier incident or what just happened. No words are needed. The love we share knows no bounds. It was an argument and amazing fucking make-up sex. The next sixty years have never looked better.

Chapter Twenty-Two

iden

I can't fucking resist her. It's just not possible. All my wife needs to do is shake her ass against my crotch and I'm ripping her clothes off. Hell, all she needs to do isbreathe and I want to rip her clothes off. At first, I thought maybe it was just that she's finally mine. She's my wife, but after thinking it over, I realize that's not it. I have always been this way with Hales. Anytime she is near me, I want to be inside her. It has nothing to do with her title in my life, or what she's wearing, or where we are. It's simply just Hailey. She owns me.

After our morning adventure, we spent the majority of the day unpacking her things from the condo. Now, we are at the grocery store. It's still new to me to be recognized by complete strangers and have them ask for my autograph. I'm just me, Aiden Emerson. Yes, I play for the League, and it's the coolest fucking job ever, but I'm just me. The only thing spectacular about me is the woman beside me, my wife.

I see Hales struggle with it too. I know it's hard for her when women throw themselves at me right in front of her. Hell, the team released an official press release and wedding photos. If they know who I am, they know I just married the love of my life. It's a shame these women have no self-respect.

Walking through the aisles, Hailey and I are both throwing things in the cart. I wasn't kidding when I told her the kitchen was bare. We ordered pizza in for lunch. "Babe, why don't you go pick up the meat for tonight and I'll finish with everything else?" she suggests.

Leaning down, I drop a kiss on her temple. "Sounds good, Mrs. Emerson," I say, then head my way to the meat department.

At the end of the aisle, I'm stopped by a little boy who is probably around eight years old. His mom tells me he's my biggest fan. I bend down and talk to him for a few minutes and then sign his shirt and a piece of paper his mom finds in her purse. By the time I make it to the meat department, the line is forever long. I'm glad Hales suggested we split up. The thought of spending hours in the grocery store does not appeal to me.

I'm standing in line, minding my own business, and scrolling through my ESPN app. My hat is pulled down low to try to avoid fans. Don't get me wrong, I'm grateful, but today I just want to be Aiden. I just want to be the husband who is at the grocery store with his wife. Unfortunately, this is not my reality.

"Excuse me," a blonde girl says as she rest her hand on my arm. "Are you Aiden Emerson?" she asks sweetly. She bats her eyelashes, trying to appear innocent, but I can see this girl is a groupie. My eyes snap to her hand on my arm before I pick it up with my hand and remove it.

"I am," I say before turning back to my phone. This girl pissed me off as soon as she touched me. It wasn't an 'I'm a huge fan; can I shake your hand?' It was an 'I'm easy and see dollar signs and fame.' I'm not fucking interested.

"Wow, you are so much hotter in person. Can I have your autograph?" she asks as she moves closer to me, pressing her fake chest against my arm.

I step to the side. I'm seething mad that this chick just thinks she can rub up on me. I close my eyes and take a deep breath, willing myself to have the patience to deal with her. When I open my eyes, I see my lifeline walking toward me. She's pushing our overflowing cart and she's beautiful. She's right behind blondie. "Hey, baby," I say to her. She smiles and her eyes flash to blondie.

"Ma'am," I say to blondie. I can see I've pissed her off. Good. "Let me get a sharpie from my beautiful wife and I would be happy to sign an autograph for you."

Hailey stops beside me with the cart and I reach for her, pulling her into my side. I kiss the top of her head. I continue to ignore blondie, but I hear her grunt as if me kissing my wife has pissed her off. Join the fucking club. "Baby," I say to Hales, "do you have a sharpie or a pen so I can sign an autograph for this lady?" I ask sweetly. She looks at me like I have lost my ever-loving mind, but she goes along with what I'm asking, digging in her purse. I'm thankful she didn't ask me what happened to the sharpie that was in my back pocket, which I used not twenty minutes ago when she and I were in the cereal aisle.

Hailey digs in her purse and pulls out a black sharpie. She hands it to me. I lean down and kiss her hand. "Thank you, angel."

Turning my attention to blondie, I ask, "What did you want me to sign?"

She smirks and her gaze snaps to Hales. A sinister smiles comes across her face. She reaches for her already dangerously low top and pulls it down to expose the cup of her bra. "Just sign here," she says with a wink.

I hear Hales gasp beside me. No fucking way. This bitch is out of line.

I turn my head so I am looking straight into Hailey's eyes. "This is a public establishment with small children. I would appreciate if you would cover yourself. I will not be signing your bra or any other intimate item or location. I am happy to give you my autograph, but not there. I am a happily married man. Out of respect for my wife, my marriage, and the parents with children who are currently watching you please cover yourself." I'm pissed off at the nerve of this chick, but keeping my eyes locked with Hales' help.

Blondie scoffs, "Whatever, I'm sure if she wasn't here you would be all over it. They all are."

"I'm sorry to disappoint you, but I am not a follower. I certainly will not be taking part in what you are suggesting. If my teammates choose to do so, that is their decision."

The woman in front of me in line turns to face us. "Mr. Emerson, it's a pleasure to meet you and your lovely wife. Please take my turn. I'm still undecided as to what I want," she says, smiling sweetly. Due to the way the line is set up, once we move up, blondie will no longer be beside us. I smile at this lifesaver who has just helped Hales and me out of an awkward situation.

"Thank you so much, Miss..." I hold out my hand.

"Mrs. James. My son is a freshman this year and is a big fan," she tells me.

"Can you give me your address? I'll make sure he gets some autographed items for your kindness."

Blondie stomps her foot when Hales and I trade places with Mrs. James and she storms off. Good riddance.

I turn back to Mrs. James. "Thank you so much for saving us. I was trying to be as polite as possible."

Mrs. James waves her hand in the air. "No problem. I wanted to smack her myself. I can only imagine how you felt," she says to Hailey.

Hales shrugs. "I think I'm still in shock." She reaches out her hand. "Thank you for your assistance."

Hailey and I order our meat and head to the checkout. I can't wait to get out of here and get home. There is a twelve pack of beer in this cart that has Liam's and my name all over it.

Chapter Twenty-Three

llison

Hailey and I are putting together salads while the guys are outside manning the grill. I brought chocolate cake for dessert and I cannot wait to dig in. I smile to myself. Surely I'm not having pregnancy cravings yet.

Hailey begins to tell me about their incident today at the grocery store. I've had women slip Liam their number and openly flirt with him, but never the boldness that Hales just described. "What a bitch." I blurt out. I'm angry for both of them to have to deal with the drama.

Hailey huffs out a breath. "I know. Aiden was great. He told her as nice as he could that he was happily married. I just hate the way women throw themselves at our husbands." She sits down in the barstool next to me and rests her elbows on the counter while burying her face in her hands.

I place my hand on her arm and gently squeeze. I don't say anything. She just needs to work through this.

The guys laugh and the noise travels in to us. Hailey looks up and stares out the patio door where they are. "It's just that...I just got him, you know? We fought so hard against our feelings." She turns to face me. "I just want to enjoy him, us. Tell me you know what I'm trying to say," she pleads.

"I do, Hales. I do understand, but we also have to understand that our husbands are professional athletes. We cannot control the idiots of the world like blondie, but we can believe in the love they have for us. We can trust that nothing will ever come between us. We have to support them and be understanding. This is our life now. Our husbands are in the spotlight. I know they need to know what is waiting on them at home is love and happiness. Blondie is not the competition. The blondies of the world are simply pesky gnats," I say, leaning my shoulder into hers.

Hailey laughs at my analogy. "I wonder if I can order an extra-large fly swatter?" she teases.

"Hey, I saw a bug zapper that looks like a tennis racquet at Walmart the other day. I wonder if that would rid the world of blondies," I say before falling into a fit of laughter. Hales is right there with me. This is how our husbands find us.

They walk through the patio door, both holding a plate of grilled meat that smells amazing. "What has you two so worked up?" Aiden stops to kiss Hales on the cheek.

Liam sets his plate on the counter and comes to stand behind me. He wraps his arms around my waist and rests his chin on my shoulder. His hands lay gently across my belly and he rubs softly back and forth. I don't even think he realizes he's doing it. Loving both me and our baby.

"I was just filling Allie in on the chick from the grocery store," Hailey tells Aiden.

"Crazy bitch," Aiden mutters. You can tell by the look on his face that he too is not impressed with what happened today. "I mean, really? I'm with my wife, who is standing right beside me, and the dumb bitch pulls down her shirt and asks me to sign her tits. No fucking thank you." He reaches over and pulls Hailey against his side. "Sorry you had to deal with that shit, angel."

Hailey shrugs as if it's no big deal, but it is. No one wants to watch as some floozy throws herself at your man right in front of your face. I'm surprised Hales didn't slap the bitch.

"Can we tell them now?" Liam whispers in my ear. He wanted to blurt it out as soon as we got here, but I managed to talk him out of it. I wanted to hang out with our friends and catch up before the conversation turns to nothing but baby talk. I'm actually shocked that Hales didn't notice my excitement. I guess it's a good thing she and Aiden are still distracted from today. It gave Liam and me a chance to surprise them with this.

I swivel in the barstool that I'm perched on so I can see Liam's face. He's grinning like a fool and his bottom lip is pushed out. He's pouting and he's adorable. I nod yes. "I left my purse by the door," I tell him. He smiles, kisses the top of my head and sprints to the door to grab the gifts that we picked up for Aiden and Hales. We bought two bibs. One says, "I love my aunt" and the other, "my uncle rocks." I cannot wait to see their faces when they open them.

Liam waltzes back into the kitchen and slides a small package across the island to each of them. "What's this?" Aiden asks, staring at the package.

Liam pulls me off the stool, takes my place, and tugs me back down on his lap. One hand rests protectively on my belly; the other rests on the counter. "It's just a little something from me and the missus. You have to open them at the same time," he tells them.

Hailey looks at Aiden and I can tell they are both confused as hell as to what could be in the tiny packages. Aiden picks them both up and hands Hailey hers. "Let's do this, angel. I can't take the suspense," he says with a small laugh.

Hailey takes hers and begins to count. Once she reaches three they both tear into their packages. Hailey squeals when she reads hers. "SQUEEEE. Holy shit. I'm going to be an aunt. This is awesome." She runs around the island and engulfs both of us in a hug.

Aiden joins the party and wraps his arms around all three of us. When they finally break away, I can feel tears running down my face. Aiden gently wipes them away. "You good, Allison" he asks.

I swallow back the emotion clogging my throat. "More than good." I take the tissue that Hailey offers and dab under my eyes. Aiden is still watching me; his face is filled with concern. "I'm going to be a mom. I'm going to have a family," I whisper. Aiden knows what this means to me. We have been best friends since I was ten years old. Other than Gran, Aiden and his parents were the only family I had. Now I have Liam and his family and our baby.

Liam wraps both arms around me and holds me close. Aiden smiles softly. "You're going to be an amazing mom, Allie. Luckiest damn kid ever." He's trying to lighten the mood and I appreciate it. These are tears of joy. Everything I have ever wanted is coming true. I miss my parents and Gran, but I know they are watching over me, helping my dreams come true. "Besides, the kid has the coolest aunt and uncle on the fucking planet." he cheers. We all laugh at him.

Life always seems to have a way of working out. The pain and sorrow you have to endure will eventually lead you to happiness.

Chapter Twenty-Four

H ailey

I'm going to be an aunt. "So how far along are you?" I ask Allison.

"We," Liam says sternly, "are about five weeks."

I stare at my brother. I study him. He has his hand laid protectively over Allison's belly. He was caveman over her before. I can only imagine how he's going to be now that they have a baby on the way. Dear Lord, please give Allie the strength to deal with his protective ass.

"We aren't really sure. I actually just took the test. I have an appointment next week," Allison explains. She doesn't comment on how my brother claims to know the exact moment they conceived.

"I am so freaking excited for you guys. Mom and Dad are going to freak. They have been dropping hints for grandkids since you and Liam got serious." I turn to Aiden. "This will take some of the pressure off us for a while," I tell him.

Aiden doesn't reply; he just winks at me. I know he is thinking about our wedding night. I begged him to not use protection. We could be pregnant as well. Instead of feeling scared, a jolt of excitement runs through me. It would be amazing to have our kids grow up together. Surprisingly I'm okay with that. I'm ready to embrace life with Aiden by my side.

The rest of the night is filled with laughter. We ended up playing Rock Band, which is always a hoot. The guys really get into character. Allison and I spend the majority of the night laughing at them and their antics. It's a little after eleven and Allison has yawned at least five times in the last ten minutes. Liam notices and places his guitar on the stand.

"Guys, we're going to head out. Allison is exhausted," Liam says. He reaches for Allison's hand to help her off the couch.

Aiden and I walk them to the door and hug them goodbye.

"Babe, why don't you head on up to bed? I'm just going to lock up," Aiden tells me as he smacks my ass.

I yelp in surprise and he roars with laughter. "I love having you here with me all the time. I love how this is our home." He kisses me on top of my head. "I love how you are my wife." He turns and walks away to turn off all the lights and make sure the house is locked up.

A few minutes later, Aiden walks into our room and finds me curled up under the covers. He strips down, leaving his clothes in the middle of the floor, and climbs into bed. Once he's under the covers, he reaches for me and pulls me into his chest. "You were too far away," he softly whispers.

I snuggle into his chest, soaking up his warmth. I kiss his chest just above his heart. "I love you." I feel his lips meet the top of my head.

"I love you too, angel."

We are both quiet for the longest time, wrapped in each other's arms. It's Aiden who breaks our silence. "So, we're going to have a niece or nephew." His voice is so soft that I can barely hear him.

"Yeah, I'm really excited for them." I am. Allison has always said she just wanted to find love and have a family. She grew up without her parents and her dream was to build her own family. My brother is making that dream come true. Although from the look on his face tonight, he is just as stoked about this baby as she is. I smile just thinking about Liam and his protectiveness with Allison.

"He's going to be a bear." Aiden chuckles. I can feel the rumble of his laughter through his chest as my head still rest against his heart.

"I know. Poor Allie. He's going to drive her nuts."

"She'll love every minute of it. This is what she's always wanted," he tells me.

I feel his hands gently tracing my spine. He places his other hand on my hip, tugging me closer to him. "Angel, that could be us," he says. I can hear the hesitation in his voice. We've never really talked about when we wanted to start a family. We both want kids, but it's never been a discussion as to when we would start.

I lift up so I can see his eyes. "Yeah," I say. I watch as my words sink in. A slow smile crosses his face.

"You're okay with that. I mean, if we get pregnant, you're good?" he stumbles over his words. I'm not sure if he's nervous because he's not okay with it or excited because he is.

"Of course. I know we've never really discussed when we would start a family, but I want to embrace life with you. I want it all." My eyes never leave his. I watch him closely, trying to decipher how he feels. The next thing I know, I'm flipped over on my back with Aiden on top of me. My legs automatically open for him as he settles in between my thighs.

He kisses my eyes, my nose, and my cheeks. My entire face is covered with small wet kisses. By the time he's done, I'm laughing uncontrollably. Aiden leans down and places his forehead against mine, cutting off my laughter. "I want to make babies with you. You let me know when you're ready, angel. I want it all. Everything life has to offer. I want it with you."

I wrap my legs around his waist and pull him to me. His length slides into me, no barrier, just Aiden. "Now," I tell him as I rock my hips against his.

"Now," he breathes as his lips seek mine in one of the deepest, most loving kisses we've ever shared.

Chapter Twenty-Five

L iam

Today is Allie's first doctor's appointment and I'm nervous as hell. Why? I have no idea. I look over at my wife and she is calm, cool, and collected. Her smile lights up her face as she stares out the window and watches the clouds go by. I love that she's happy. I would do anything to make sure that smile is plastered on her face every single day.

I pull into the lot and put the car in park. Allison turns to face me. "You got us here forty-five minutes early, silly man," she says, laughing.

Yes, I wanted to leave early. I didn't want to get stuck in traffic and I wanted to make sure we were on time. I didn't want to miss the appointment. I need Allie to see the doctor today so she can reassure me that everything is okay, that my wife and my baby are healthy. Irrational, yes, I know. Do I care? No, I don't. Nothing is more important to me.

"I just didn't want to be late," I say. I don't want to tell her how nervous I am. Just the thought of something happening to either one of them has me on edge. If my calculations are correct, our baby will be here in November, right in the heat of the season. I've read that long trips are not recommended at that stage of pregnancy. I've also read that planned deliveries can also happen. Maybe we can do it on a home game week. I have to be there. No, I need to be there. I'm scared shitless that I won't be.

The receptionist greets us with a smile. This is Allie's doctor so we don't have a ton of paperwork to fill out. To my surprise, we are called back to a room rather quickly. When I mention this to the nurse, she tells me she always does that for Allie and patients who are in our similar status of popularity. It helps with confidentiality. This also eases my mind. Being in the spotlight of the League, I worry about who is out to make a buck. It's good to know Allie's healthcare and that of our baby's is being safeguarded and the staff is helping to take extra precaution.

After checking her vitals, the nurse hands Allie a gown and a sheet, advising her to change and drape the sheet over her lap. I don't question the process. I assume it's so they can do an ultrasound and see how far along she is. I'm not sure how low on her belly they need to go, but I'm sure her jeans will be in the way.

Not ten minutes later, still way ahead of our appointment time, there is a knock on the door. The door opens and in walks the doctor who is, to my surprise, a man. What the fuck? I look at Allie and she politely smiles at the doctor as he begins asking her how she's feeling. I shake my head and focus back on the conversation. It's hard though; I don't want another man touching her, not even her doctor. I can tell Allison is comfortable with him. I bite back my unjustified anger and focus on what he's saying.

He goes over her vitals that were taken by the nurse and tells her everything looks great. He also informs her that he will do bloodwork before we leave. After a few more questions asking about morning sickness and diet, the doctor sets his computer to the side and washes his hands. He approaches the table and folds down Allie's blanket and pulls up her gown, exposing her belly. I growl in response and they both look at me.

"Mr. MacCoy, I'm just going to examine your wife. This will be quick, and then I will have the nurse bring in the sonogram machine. If what you are telling me is correct, Allison is not far enough along to hear your baby's heartbeat through the Doppler, but we can see it with an ultrasound." This causes my earlier irritation to be pushed aside as I stare into the eyes of my beautiful girl. She has tears in her eyes. Leaning down, I say for her ears only, "We get to see our baby today," and kiss her on the cheek. I catch the lone tear that falls from those beautiful eyes with my thumb.

The doctor leaves to ask the nurse to bring in the sonogram machine. Allie turns her head to face me. "Liam, I can't believe this is happening. We're having a baby," she says in awe. With those words, I fall a little more in love with her. Every single day I fall deeper in love with my wife. It's a feeling like nothing I have ever known.

A few minutes later, another knock sounds at the door to alert us it's time to see our baby. The nurse wheels in the machine and sets it up, while the doctor asks Allison to please place her feet in the stirrups on the bed. I raise my eyebrows in question, but I don't say anything. I've already had one outward moment of jealousy. I'm trying to keep my shit in check for my girl.

I watch as the nurse sets up the machine and nods to the doctor that she's ready. I watch as she hands him a wand looking contraption with a condom on the end of it. It looks like a fucking sex toy. "What the hell is that?" I blurt out. All eyes are now on me.

"Mr. MacCoy, due to the fact that your wife is in the very early stages of her pregnancy, a traditional ultrasound will not show us what we need to see. We will be performing a transvaginal ultrasound today."

The only words I caught were performing and vaginal. Nope, not gonna happen. "I don't think so," I tell him. I tighten my grip on Allison's hand.

"Liam," she says in a soft calming voice.

I turn to face her and she cups my cheek with her hand. "Baby, this has to happen. This is not much different than the exams I get for my birth control. We get to see our baby," she says again, trying to soothe me.

I'm not an idiot. I know she has to be examined, but in my mind, her doctor was always a woman. The thought of another man seeing her. I bite down hard on my bottom lip to keep from lashing out. I pull in a few deep breaths to calm my nerves. "I know, but I always just assumed your doctor was female. You know, female problems, female doctor," I say. Even as the words leave my mouth, I know I sound irrational, but this my Allie. When have I ever been rational when it comes to her?

"Mr. MacCoy," the doctor breaks in, "I can assure you that this is strictly a medical procedure to ensure that your wife and baby are doing well." He watches me closely for a reaction.

Allison squeezes my hand. "Liam?" Her voice a whisper.

My chest deflates with resignation as I nod yes, giving the doctor the go ahead to continue. I need to keep my jealous ass in check. This is for the baby. I just have to keep repeating that over and over in my head until this damn *procedure* is done.

Chapter Twenty-Six

iden

A week. That's how long it's been since my wife and I decided we would stop using protection and try to start a family. It's also been an equal amount of time that I stopped thinking with my brain and let my dick rule. On our wedding night, I made love to Hales with nothing between us. It happened once, and it will be a night and an experience that I will always remember. However, the last week has been pure bliss. I cannot get enough of her, of being inside of her with nothing between us. The entire experience of sex has changed for me. The way she feels wrapped around me, the warmth, I can't fucking get my fill of her.

I think we've had sex on every surface of this house at least once. We are working on our second round. Hell, the other day we went out for ice cream and I spent the entire time watching as her tongue licked at her cone. As soon as we got home, I pulled into the garage, and hit the button to lower the door. Hailey met me at my side of the car. I picked her up and she instantly wrapped herself around me. I took her against the wall in the garage. I couldn't wait one more second to be inside of her. That's pretty much been our life this past week.

Not only has the time with my wife been great, but being with her all the time, I love it. The sex is also amazing, off the charts amazing. It gets better each time. I'm also pretty sure we are pregnant. Hell, I don't know how we're not.

We haven't told anyone that we are trying or not actively trying to prevent getting pregnant. Hailey said she didn't want to take away from Liam and Allison's news, but I know they would be stoked for us. A smile spreads across my face thinking about our kids growing up together. Everything finally seems to be falling into place for all of us.

"AIDEN." Hailey yells my name. I'm downstairs watching ESPN and she's upstairs, at least that how it sounded. I jump off the couch and run up the steps to make sure she's okay.

"What's up, angel?" I ask as I enter our bedroom.

I see the bathroom light is on, but the door is closed. I knock on the door. "Hales, baby, you okay?" I ask, concerned.

"Am I okay? Really, Aiden? How many fucking times do I have to ask you to replace the damn toilet paper roll when you use the last of it? I have to sit down to pee, not just to shit, and toilet paper is an essential part of that process," she seethes.

Oops. I used the last of it this morning and forgot to get another roll from the closet. The closet that is located on the other side of the bathroom. She either has to drip dry or stand up and let it drip as she gets another roll. "Look at the bright side. At least I'm here and you're not home alone," I tell her.

"Just get me some damn toilet paper." she yells through the door. I smash my lips together to keep from laughing. If she sees that, she's really going to be pissed. Just my luck, she would punish me by cutting me off, and she's like crack, my addiction. No way can I let that happen.

I get myself under control and turn the handle. Hailey is sitting on the toilet, arms crossed, scowling at me. I bite down hard on my bottom lip to keep from laughing. She looks fucking adorable sitting there pouting. I grab two rolls of TP. I hand one to her and sit the other on the back of the tank, just in case I forget the next time. You would think this would make her happy. Yeah, not so much.

"You can go," she says, not even bothering to look at me. She's really pissed off about this.

"Hales," I say, my voice gentle.

"GAH. Get out." She throws the roll of TP at my head. I duck, barely missing the soft cotton roll.

I don't try to calm her down; instead, I leave the bathroom, shutting the door behind me. I sit on the bed and patiently wait for her to finish her business. I smile at the thought of her chucking the roll at my head. It's a good thing I grabbed two or she would have been in the same predicament. Somehow, I don't think she would appreciate me pointing that out.

When she finally emerges from the bathroom, she appears to be calmed down. She walks to her dresser and pulls out a pair of socks. I can't stand it when she's mad at me, so I slowly rise from the bed and step behind her. I place both of my hands on her shoulders and begin to massage her muscles. She leans her head forward, allowing me to work. I can feel her relax underneath my hands.

Without warning, I scoop down and lift her into my arms. I carry her to the bed and lay her down, climbing in beside her. We lie facing each other. I tuck a loose tendril of hair behind her ear. "I'm sorry, angel." Hales doesn't ask for much, and replacing the TP is the least I can do. I'm just so used to it just being me. I love her being here, and I love being married, but there is still an adjustment phase. "I'll try harder," I say. I don't offer an excuse.

She's quiet for a while, her eyes closed as I gently stroke her hair. "I may have overreacted, but damn it, Emerson, you can be so frustrating. I could hear you laughing at me," she pouts.

Pouting is a good sign. This means she's no longer pissed off and I am on my way to being back in her good graces. Make-up sex sounds pretty damn good to me right now. Who am I kidding? Sex with Hales anytime, anywhere, any type sounds good all the time.

She leans forward and kisses me. Just a small chaste kiss, but that's all it takes to light my desire for her. "I'm sorry too," she says.

That's what I needed, those words. I know she's over it and I can take what's mine. I pull her against me. "What do you say we go for another practice run?" I say, kissing her neck.

She smirks as she pushes me onto my back and climbs on top. My wife is amazing.

Chapter Twenty-Seven

Allison

Liam is squeezing my hand so tight; I think he might be cutting off my circulation. I don't dare tell him. I'm actually surprised at how well he has behaved considering my male physician and the vaginal ultrasound he is about to perform. It was touch and go a couple of times with his overprotective tendencies. I smile. I can't wait to tell Hales about this. She will get a kick out of her brother's obvious jealousy.

I place my feet in the stirrups and slide to the end of the exam table like I'm told. I've never had this done before, but it can't be worse than a yearly exam. Besides, this time I get to see my baby.

"All right, Allison, I want you to guide this in for me so we ensure you are comfortable." I'm shocked that I am going to have to do this, but really, it makes sense. I mean, I can feel what I'm doing; he cannot. Liam is tense beside me. I offer him a smile to let him know I'm good.

I take the wand from the doctor and do as he says and "guide" it in. This is a very uncomfortable situation. First of all, it's embarrassing to have to "guide" anything into myself. Second, my husband is seconds away from going bat shit crazy on my doctor.

Once I'm in, the doctor takes over with the wand. His hand is under the blanket, and Liam's eyes are glued to it. My eyes are glued on Liam. It not until I hear the doctor say "there" do I turn my attention to the monitor that is sitting beside the exam table.

On the small black and white screen, I seen a tiny black blob that is flickering fast. My heart is pounding. I've read enough to know that I'm not far enough along in my pregnancy to actually make out body parts, but regardless, that's our baby.

"This," the doctor points to the screen with his free hand, "is your baby. The flickering you see, that's the heartbeat. Nice and strong," he says. I feel tears running down my face, and then Liam's lips. He's kissing my cheek.

"That's our baby, beautiful girl. I love you so fucking much." he says for all ears to hear. I can hear the doctor and nurse chuckle. Gone is Mr. Overprotective. Now sits a man with glassy eyes and a big goofy grin. I watch as a lone tear escapes. I reach up and gently wipe it away. "We made that," he says in awe.

I love this man. Never in my life did I think I could find this, happiness and a man who loves me with everything in him. Today is yet another memory that I will hold near to my heart for the rest of my life.

"It looks as though you are right at six weeks along. This gives you a due date of early November," the doctor explains.

Liam stands up and kisses me, a kiss full of love. I don't notice the physician and the nurse have turned off the machine and the "wand" is no longer a part of the equation. It's just my husband, Liam. He's all I see. The sound of the exam room door opening brings me back to reality and I pull away from Liam's kiss. The doctor is standing there with an amused look on his face. He hands Liam a bag.

"Inside you will find a DVD recording of today's ultrasound so you can watch it anytime you choose. There are also several printed pictures." He turns to look at me. "There is a folder in the bag that has brochures on this stage of pregnancy as well as diet tips and tips for morning sickness. I know you have had no symptoms, some never do and some do about this time. I have also included a prescription for prenatal vitamins that you will need to take on a daily basis." He types something on his computer, then places it back on the counter. "Do you have any questions?"

"Yes," Liam clears his throat. "Is it okay to have sex? Will we hurt the baby?" he asks. You can hear the concern in his voice. He's going to be such an amazing father. I already know the answer, but I let the doctor ease Liam's mind.

"Yes, sexual intercourse is perfectly fine. There is no chance of you hurting your baby," he says kindly.

Liam nods that he heard the answer, but he doesn't speak.

"Thank you, doctor," I reply for him.

"Allison, we will see you back in four weeks, unless you need us before then," he says as he walks out the door.

Once the door is closed, I climb off the exam table and begin to take off my gown. Apparently, it's me being naked that snaps my husband out of his trance. I feel his hands on my waist and he moves in behind me. "Allison MacCoy, you are amazing," he says against my ear. Goose bumps break out against my skin.

"I love you, Liam."

"Baby, you don't even know. I can't even find the words to tell you how amazing this is. To see our baby." He spins me around and drops to his knees. He places gentle kisses all over my bare stomach. "We made that, Allie." The awe is his voice has tears again falling down my cheeks.

I run my fingers through his hair. He looks up and our eyes meet. "Yes, we did." He stands and his lips capture mine. He kisses me until I'm weak in the knees and gasping for air.

"Let's get you dressed, beautiful. We have some news to share." He helps me dress and leads me out to the car.

As soon as we are in the car, he dials his phone. Aiden answers. I can't hear his reply when Liam asks him if we can stop by, but I can tell by the direction that we are driving that we are, indeed, stopping by.

Chapter Twenty-Eight

H‌ailey

Aiden and I are lounging around today. It's raining and dreary, so we have been curled up on the couch watching television. Aiden's phone rings and I can hear it's my brother on the other end. I can't make out what he's saying, but I hear Aiden tell them to stop by anytime, that we will be home all day. Today was Allison's doctor's appointment. I hope they have good news for us.

Aiden ends the call. "That was Liam. He wanted to know if they could stop by."

"Yeah, today was Allison's appointment," I remind him.

"He sounded off. I hope everything's okay," he tells me. Liam sounding off is not a good sign. I can imagine my brother bursting at the seams at the news that he and Allison are going to be parents. I know there are a lot of false positive home tests. I try not to worry until I can hear from them what happened.

I curl into Aiden's side and he wraps his arms around me as we wait for them to arrive. Twenty minutes later, there is a knock at the door.

We both go to the door to greet them. When Aiden pulls open the door, Liam and Allison are standing there. He's holding her tight against his side with one arm while the others carries a white bag with a medical logo on it. I can't tell from their facial expressions what's going on. We step back and allow them to come in. Aiden leads the way to the living room. He sits down on the couch and pulls me onto his lap. Liam sits on the other end and does the same with Allison.

"What's in the bag?" Aiden asks.

Liam pulls out a DVD and hands it to him. "Do you mind throwing this in?" he asks. Still, I can't tell what's going on and I'm too afraid to ask them.

I hop off Aiden's lap and grab the DVD. I remove it from the case and pop it into the DVD player. Grabbing the remote off the coffee table, I perch myself back on my husband's lap.

"That better not be a delivery video. I've heard about that shit. I don't want any part of it unless it's Hales," Aiden says. He's serious as a heart attack and we all laugh at him. His little outburst helps ease some of my tension. I'm still concerned and these two are giving nothing away.

Liam grabs the remote out of my hands and hits play. All eyes are glued to the flat screen as a black and white screen appears. I see Allison's name and the date at the top. When my eyes finally find the center of the screen I see a black blob that is flickering fast. There is an arrow pointing that says "baby."

"Holy shit," Aiden says. "Is that...is that your baby?" His voice is gruff. I turn to look at him and his eyes are locked on the screen, a silly smile on his face.

I turn my gaze to my brother and sister-in-law. Their matching smiles are blinding. Allison squeals and stands up. I mimic her and we embrace and jump up and down like crazed fools. I'm going to be an aunt.

I hear Aiden congratulate Liam. Then I feel him behind me. He gently picks me up and moves me out of the way so he can offer her a congratulatory hug. Before I can register what's happening, my brother has me in his arms spinning me in circles. "I'm going to be a dad. We're having a baby," he cheers and his enthusiasm is infectious.

Liam finally lowers me to the floor and I trade places with Allison. "Congratulations, guys. I'm so happy for you," I tell them as I wipe the tears from my eyes.

"We're due in November," Liam tells us. I see him lose a little of the happiness. I know my brother. He's afraid he's going to miss it. He's already hating the fact that he will be on the road so much at the time the baby is due.

"Don't worry. You are looking at a highly trained labor and delivery nurse. I will be glued to her side the entire time you are away," I tell him.

I watch as his shoulders relax at my words. Silly man, she's going to be just fine. So is that little bundle she's carrying.

Aiden and I decided we were going to wait to tell them or anyone really that we are trying. Apparently, he forgot about the entire conversation from the words that fly out of his mouth.

"We're trying, too," he says with a huge grin. He places his hands on my belly as he stands behind me. He has the same exact hold of me as Liam does Allison.

"Really?" Allison screeches and launches herself at me. "That's so awesome. Our kids can grow up together. This is the best news ever. I didn't think that this day could get any better," she says. My anxiety that our news would be taking away from their moment fades away at her words.

"I didn't want to say anything yet," I confess.

"What? Why?" Allison asks, confused.

"I just didn't want to take away from your news. I'm so freaking happy for your guys."

"Never," Allison says with conviction. "This is even better. I never had cousins growing up. It wasn't until I moved in with Gran and met Aiden that I had other kids around. I am ecstatic that our kids will grow up together." She hugs me again, tighter this time.

"All right, easy now. She's carrying precious cargo," Liam chides.

Allie and I laugh at his antics. "You think that's bad. Let me tell you about the appointment." She proceeds to tell us about their appointment and my overbearing brother. Nothing stops him when it comes to his beautiful girl.

Chapter Twenty-Nine

L iam

I want to shout it from the fucking rooftops. I knew I wanted kids, and Allie and I would take that step. What I didn't know was how fucking incredible it would feel to see that tiny little blip on the screen. I can't find the words to describe it. Allie is twelve weeks today. We have invited my parents, as well as Aiden, Hales, and the Emersons, over for dinner. If I don't get to tell someone else, I'm going to burst.

Two weeks ago, Allie had her second appointment and we got to hear the heartbeat. A grown man should not cry as much as I have in the last few months. Frommarrying the woman of my dreams to starting our family, my man card is in serious jeopardy. Allie just laughs and says I should be puffing out my chest and bragging that I knocked her up on our honeymoon. It's hard to believe it happened that fast since she just stopped taking her birth control. The doctor just said it's easier for some women to conceive than others. Thank the Lord, my girl has an easy time of it. I have to admit the act of trying was fun, but really, nothing has changed. Allison has felt great and our sex life is still un-fucking-believable. No complaints from me.

Allison went all out with dinner. She made baby back ribs, baby carrots, and baby red potatoes. She also made white cupcakes with pink and blue icing. She went all out. It's going to be hard to not blurt it out, but she wants to see how long it will take them to figure it out. She also bought each of them grandparent bibs, the same as we did with Aiden and Hales, just in case dinner does not clue them in. She's glowing from her pregnancy. So far, she has felt great, no sickness. We couldn't be happier.

Aiden and Hailey are the first to arrive. Allison fills them in on the plan with dinner to see if they can figure it out. She also tells them about the bibs, just in case they don't figure it out. Both agree to not let the cat out of the bag and see how long it takes for the subtle hints to register.

By the time my parents and the Emersons arrive, dinner is ready. Hailey gets the door while Aiden and I carry everything to the table. I don't want Allie lifting anything. I know it's not that heavy and I'm being overprotective once again, but there is no reason for her to do it when Aiden and I are both here. Allison just rolls her eyes and smiles as she tells us what needs taken to the dining room and what doesn't. My girl is used to me; she knows I'm stubborn. I like to think she loves me because of it.

Once the hello hugs are passed out, we gather around and dig in. Not one of them mentions the "baby" theme of the meal. I watch Allison. She has a soft smile gracing her lips. I know she wants them to notice. I'm glad she went ahead and got the bibs, just in case. It appears they are too wrapped up in the deliciousness of the meal to pick up on her subtle hint.

We make it through dinner without a word being said. I clear off the table with Aiden's help. We send everyone else on into the living room with the promise that we will bring dessert to them. Instead of loading the dishwasher, I place everything in the sink and put the food away. The suspense as to if they will get the next hint is killing me. I'll get to the dishes later. With Aiden's help, it takes no time to wrap up the leftovers; of course, there were not many. My wife in an amazing cook. She also loves to bake, so cupcakes will be no surprise to our family. It will have to be the colors that tip them off; otherwise, it's moving on to plan B.

I carry in the cupcakes and sit them on the coffee table. Dad and Mr. Emerson dig in. They can never resist my girl's baked goods. Conversation continues to flow with no talk about what we are trying to tell them. Finally, I can't take it anymore. I nod to Hailey and she grabs the four small wrapped gifts from the hall closet. She hands them to Allison who is sitting on my lap where she belongs.

It's like this is the first time my mom really looks at us. "Allison, you're glowing. Married life suits you," she says sweetly. It takes all I have not to yell, "I knocked her up," but I don't. I want to see their faces when they open the bibs.

Allison hands one to each of them. Pink for the moms and blue for the dads. Each contains a bib pertaining to grandparents. The Emersons are not technically Allie's parents, but they are the closest thing she has. There is not a single doubt in my mind that they will not treat our baby just as equally as they will Aiden's and Hailey's.

All four of their faces are masked with confusion. "Open them," I say, gesturing to the packages in their hands. They remind me of kids at Christmas as they tear into the paper. All at once, I hear a collective gasp. All eyes turn to face us. "Surprise." I say as I pull Allison back against my chest and rest my hand on her belly.

"Is this for real?" my mom asks. It's like she's afraid to believe it. I nod at Aiden who is sitting in the chair opposite ours with Hailey in his lap. He has the remote in hand, ready to push play, which he does.

The screen fills with the black and white image of our baby. The little tiny blip, our first video/photo of our peanut.

Once it sets in, we are all on our feet for congratulatory hugs and handshakes. Mom and Mrs. Emerson are both crying, so are Allie and Hales.

It's Mr. Emerson who finally figures it out. "Baby back ribs, baby carrots, and baby potatoes," he says and we all start to laugh.

"Blue and pink cupcakes," my dad replies.

"We had to go to plan B since our subtle hints were not getting through," I say, laughing at them.

Mr. Emerson turns to Aiden. "You knew," he says.

Aiden nods yes. "So when are we going to get one of these from you?" he asks, and suddenly all eyes are on Hales and Aiden. I'm going to enjoy watching him wiggle his way out of this one. I don't think anyone else knows they are trying.

Chapter Thirty

 iden

My heart begins to race and my palms are sweaty at my dad's question. My eyes seek out my wife. She was sure we would be pregnant right away considering she wasn't taking birth control. Allie and Liam were able to right away and Hales was sure that we would too. Here we are several weeks later and still waiting for it to happen. When her eyes meet mine, she gives me a small nod, letting me know she's okay with us telling them we, too, are trying to have a baby. I'm good with telling them, but I need her in my arms when I do.

I walk to the other side of the room where she is standing with her mom, mine, and Allie. I pull her into my side as close as I can get her. My eyes stay locked with hers as I answer my dad's question. "Actually, we're trying," I say.

It takes about two seconds before Mom and Mrs. MacCoy tackle hug us like they did with Allie and Liam. These ladies are really excited to become grandparents. Dad and Mr. MacCoy both shake my hand and kiss Hales on the cheek.

Hales and I both smile through the congratulations, but I know she's worried it will never happen for us. I try to reassure her that these things can take time; at least, that's what the book I bought says. Liam said he read it and it was very informative about changes and what to expect. I've learned a lot, including it takes time and stress can keep it from happening. Hales is stressed. It's like as soon as we decided that we were going to try, she expected it to be right away. She's a nurse. I know she knows better, but it's different when it's you. All of your training goes out the window.

I'm going to talk to Liam before we leave. I think we need to send the girls on a spa day. Hales needs some girl time and maybe Allison can help ease her fears.

After our parents calm down, we enjoy spending time with each other. The guys split off and talk about the upcoming season. The girls are engrossed in all things baby talk. My heart hurts for Hales. I can see her smile, but her eyes are telling a different story. Even from across the room, I can see the longing. Last night, lying in bed, she said she never knew how bad she wanted to be a mom and to share that with me until she felt like she might not be able to. Again, I tried to reassure her it's only been two months; these things take time.

Finally, our parents leave. I've been wanting to talk to Liam. He's not only my brother-in-law, but he's my best friend. I'm hoping he can help me out with Hales.

"So, Hales is stressing over us not being pregnant yet." I decide to just get it out there.

"You can see it in her eyes," is his reply. It's almost a relief that he sees it too, that I'm not just making shit up in my head to justify her being sad. "Did you pick up that book I was telling you about?"

"Yeah, I even showed it to her. Fuck, man, she's a nurse who assists with delivering babies. She knows it takes time. She just really wants it," I tell him.

Liam eyes me carefully. "What about you? Do you want it?" he asks. I don't blame him. If it was Allison and the roles were reversed, I would ask the same question.

"I do, man. More than I thought possible. I want everything with her. The entire package. There's nothing I wouldn't do to make her happy."

"I know. I get it, trust me." He takes a drink of his beer. "I don't know why it happened so fast for us. I know it will happen for you guys though. You deserve to feel this," he says. It's then I realize he is holding a sonogram picture. "I can't stop looking at it. I freak out when she leaves the house. I just want to put her in a bubble so I can keep them both safe."

Liam has always been overprotective of Allison; however, I see his point. It's taking Hales and me some time to get there, but I can see myself being a little irrational at times worrying about her and the baby. "I just...I want it to happen just as bad as she does. I try not to talk about it and show too much excitement because I don't want to put more stress on her. I know it will happen. She's just...."

"She just wants instant gratification. That's Hales. She's always been that way. Just stay strong and be there for her. Enjoy the practice." He winks at me. It took a while for us to be able to discuss sex and Hales in the same conversation. After all, she is his little sister.

"You're right about that. I have to admit, the practice is definitely not a hardship. Fuck, man, I have no clue how she's not pregnant. We've been going at it like rabbits. I was sure that first week would have sealed the deal for us," I say as I swallow back the rest of my beer so we can join the girls in the living room.

Their heads turn at the sound of the door opening. Liam settles on the oversized chair with Allison, while I join Hales on the couch. It's then that Liam speaks up. I swear he can read my mind. "Baby, Aiden and I thought it would be nice for you and Hales to have a day at the spa. What do you think?" he asks her. He's making it sound like it's all about her, and I know he wants her relaxed, but I also know the reason he's wording it this way is so Hales will go along with it. He's a genius who reads minds.

"That actually sounds great. It's been a while since we've had a girls' day," Allison replies. "What do you think, Hales?"

"Spa day? Do you even have to ask? Hell yeah I'm in." My wife lights up with excitement.

I breathe a sigh of relief. Maybe this will help her relax. Then when she gets home, we can get back to practicing.

Chapter Thirty-One

A llison

When Liam suggested Hales and I have a spa day, I wondered why I hadn't thought of it. I miss her. We hang out a lot as couples, but it's been a while since she and I just took a day to spend together. I called first thing this morning and they were able to work us in. Of course, I'm sure the fact that we are married to two League players had nothing to do with it. Usually, Hales and I both refrain from using our names and our husbands for special treatment, but in this case, I played it up. Even guaranteed the guys would be dropping us off and picking us up. I knew I would have no trouble convincing them to do so. Liam has been up my ass since the day we found out I was pregnant. More so now than ever. I know he's just being the loving, doting, overprotective husband that he is, but at times it can be stifling.

That's part of the reason why I am so excited for some girl time. I love Liam with everything in me, but he still annoys me at times and I know Hales will know exactly what I'm talking about and share a few of her own beefs that she has with Aiden. Needless to say, I am super excited for our day at the spa.

"Hey," Hailey says into the phone.

"Hey. I just got off the phone with the spa. They were more than accommodating for Mrs. MacCoy and Mrs. Emerson to be joining them today." I laugh into the phone.

Hailey giggles. "So what time did they fit us in?" she asks.

"I booked us for one o'clock and we're getting the works. I did tell them that our husbands would be dropping us off," I admit.

"That's awesome. Maybe they might want to join us for a couples massage," Hailey suggests.

No way. "Not this time. I am missing out on my girl time. It's you and me today, chick," I tell her.

"I was hoping you would say that. I just wanted to put it out there," she laughs.

"Okay, well, we will see you in a few hours. Tell Aiden to blame me." I laugh into the phone.

"See you then."

I hit end on my cell phone as two strong arms wrap around me. My husband immediately cradles my belly with his big strong hands. "You all set for your spa day, beautiful?"

"Yeah, Hales seems to be looking forward to it. They worked us right in as soon as they found out who our husbands were. I did have to mention that the two of you would be dropping us off." I turn my head slightly so I can see his face. He offers me a warm, loving smile.

"I was going to drive you anyway," he says with a wink.

"Of course you were," I say dryly. I remove his hands from my belly and walk out of his embrace. He reaches out to pull me back in, but I stop him with the glare I'm sending him. "Liam. Damn it. I'm pregnant, not dying. The doctor says I am perfectly healthy. You don't have to hover over me all the damn time."

My outburst surprises both of us. I have always loved any time that I can spend with Liam. He's my best friend, my soul mate, but these last few weeks I cannot even take a shower without him coming upstairs to check on me. I know he loves me and our baby, but he has got to get a grip. Maybe it's the pregnancy hormones, but I don't think so.

"Allie, I'm sorry. I'm not trying to control you. I just need to know the two of you are safe. God, if something happened to you," he moves to stand in front of me and drops to his knees, lifting my shirt, he kisses my small baby bump, "or you," he whispers. "I can't live without you. I need to make sure you are healthy and safe." He stands back up and guides me to the couch. He sits down and pulls me onto his lap.

I turn so I am straddling his hips; we are now face to face. I place both hands on either side of his face and study him. "Talk to me." My voice is soft. I can see the worry in his eyes and I don't get it. I'm healthy, the doctor said so.

Liam pulls me into his chest and releases a heavy sigh. "I'm afraid I'm going to miss something." We sit like that, holding each other for several minutes. Finally, I pull away. I don't say anything. I need him to talk to me.

"Not only do I have this urge to protect you, I have this feeling that something is going to happen and I'm not going to be here. During training camp I will be gone for four weeks. Four fucking weeks, Allison. What if you need me? You will be here at night by yourself." He places one hand on my belly. "I don't want to miss a minute of this. That's part of me growing inside of you. That's amazing and beautiful, and I want to remember every damn minute of it, but I can't. I won't be here. I know I sound irrational, but add that to this feeling that something is going to happen...I'm a fucking mess."

I lean in to kiss his lips. Just a small tender kiss to let him know I'm right here. "Liam, babe, nothing is going to happen. During training camp, you can still see me; we can Skype," I say, rubbing my belly. "It's all going to be okay."

"What happens if you go into labor and we are on the road for a game? I cannot miss the birth of my child," he says, panic in his voice.

This really is worrying him. "I talked to my doctor. If the pregnancy is going well and there are no complications—" I lift my hand to stop him from speaking. "The doctor has assured me everything is going perfectly. If that continues, we can discuss scheduling the delivery. They would induce my labor, so we can plan for you being in town. It's not a definite, but he assured me it's completely safe for the baby and me."

Liam wrinkles his brow, seeming to really think about what I just told him. "I read that they can do that. Is It safe? For both of you?" he fires off his round of questioning.

"Yes, yes, yes, and yes. Babe, it's all going to be okay." I lean down and rest my forehead against his. "I love you, Liam MacCoy."

His arms grip me tight, holding me against him. "I love you too, beautiful girl."

Chapter Thirty-Two

H ailey

Aiden and I pull into the spa a few minutes before one. He had no problem with driving me. I knew he wouldn't. I felt bad asking him though. These past few weeks, I've been distant with him. I'm stressing over getting pregnant. I didn't realize how badly I wanted a baby until that first month and the negative test. My heart was crushed. My amazing husband just held me and told me it would happen for us. Allison got pregnant so fast; I was sure I would as well. I know as a nurse that these things take time, but when it's you, when you want it so bad, all that knowledge and reasoning flies out the window.

Aiden gets out of the car, but I don't wait for him to open my door. He scowls at me a little and I just smile at him. He does so much for me. I can open my own damn car door. We meet at the front of the car where he immediately wraps his arm around my waist and pulls me against his chest. I feel his lips on the top of my head. This man, he's everything. My heart aches that I cannot give him a baby.

Inside the spa, I spot Liam and Allie talking to whom I assume is the manager of the spa. I watch as Liam hands back a piece of paper. Stepping up beside them, the manager turns to look at us. "Aiden Emerson," he thrusts his hand toward Aiden, "It's a pleasure to meet you. I'm Mike Jefferson. My family owns the spa." He then turns to me, reaching for my hand. "Mrs. Emerson, it's a pleasure." I smile politely and shake his hand. Inside, I am doing a happy dance at being called by my married name. I'm still adjusting to being Mrs. Aiden Emerson.

After a little small talk and Aiden signing an autograph, we say goodbye to our husbands and begin our afternoon of pampering. First up is our massage. Allison and I opted to do this in the same room, so we can catch up. I've really missed her.

We have to watch what we say in front of the massage therapist. Our husbands are professional football players. They could take what we say, spin it, and sell the story to the tabloids. This is hard for me because I really want to talk to Allie about this rift between Aiden and me. I hate feeling this distance between us.

Instead, she tells me how she and Liam got into an argument over him not putting the seat down. I swear I'm laughing so hard I'm crying. I even hear a soft chuckle from the girl who is doing my massage.

"Seriously, who wants to fall ass first into the damn toilet first thing in the morning. It's not even the first time. A few weeks prior, it was in the middle of the night. I was calm the next morning and asked him to please put the seat back down, and he agreed. Now I know he was just agreeing to appease me. UGH." Allison says, lying on the table next to me.

"I'm glad we each had our own bathroom growing up," I tell her. "You're not the only one whose husband needs training," I tell her. "The other day after using the restroom, I reached for some toilet paper and the roll was empty. Thank God I just had to pee." I proceed to tell her how Aiden laughed, but then quickly changed his tune when he saw how angry it made me. "Hell, all they have to do it whip it out and shake it dry. They just don't get it," I say, my frustration with the situation clearly evident.

Both massage therapists' chuckle at my words. Great, I can see it now. League wives complain of training husbands. This spa is used by many celebrities who are way more famous than our husbands. I just hope the staff is as great with confidentiality as they say. I tend to lose myself in conversation when it's just me and Allison. We don't get time without the guys hanging around very often.

The entire day is amazing. After our massages, we moved on to facials and ended with manicures and pedicures. I have not felt this relaxed in a long time.

"Hey, what if we call the guys and tell them we are going to be a little longer? We could run across the street to that little café and grab something to eat?" Allison asks me.

I place my arm around her shoulders as we walk toward the lobby. "I say you, my dear, are the smartest woman I know," I say with a smile.

After calling the guys and telling them where they can pick us up at in a couple of hours, we set in at a small table in the back corner of the café. There's not a large crowd, but even if there were, this table offers us privacy.

The waitress takes our order and brings our drinks. After she excuses herself, I decide to dive right in. "I can't get pregnant," I blurt out.

Allison studies me. "Hailey Emerson, what's it been? Two months?" she asks.

"Three. Three months of non-stop sex and nothing," I reply.

Allison reaches over and places her hand on top of mine. "Hales, you know these things can take time. I read in a pregnancy book that worrying about it causes more stress and your body fights against you," she explains.

"I know, but before we officially started trying, there were a few times with no stress, just us, and we still aren't," I explain.

"Hailey Emerson, do you hear yourself? You're a nurse. You know three months is not a long time to be trying to conceive. There are people who try for years and years before they have a successful pregnancy. What's really going on?" she asks.

Resting my arms on the table, I bury my face in my hands. "I don't know," I mumble. I lift my head to look at Allison. "I know I sound irrational. I do. I know everything you just said is true. I just want it now. We fought so hard to be where we are; I just want it all. I want to grab onto life with Aiden and hold on as tight as I can. I want to start our family. I want our kids to grow up together," I say, my voice cracking.

"Hailey, you have to give your body some time. You need to relax," she tries to soothe me.

"I know, damn it. I know all of that, but what if I can't, huh? What happens when I can't give Aiden the family he wants? Then what? I can't keep him tied to me in a relationship that will prevent him from being a father." I deflate at my own words, slumping my shoulders and sitting back into my chair. Aiden is amazing; he could have anyone and he chose me. I know he loves me and I love him with everything in me, but I would never be able to do that to him. "I don't want to have to walk away," I whisper, my voice thick, fighting back the tears that are threatening to fall.

"What are you—" She stops when the waitress delivers our salads. "What the hell are you talking about? Walk away?" Allison questions me. I can see hurt in her eyes at the thought of me leaving Aiden.

I take a sip of my water. "He wants this, Allie. I wish you could have seen his eyes light up when we decided to officially try. He was so excited. I could never take that away from him. If I cannot conceive, yes, I would leave him. I would file for divorce and disappear. That's the only way he could ever move on and find someone who can give him babies," I try to explain.

My eyes find Allison and she is staring at me with her mouth hanging open. "Are you fucking kidding? Do you even hear yourself right now?" she seethes. "Hailey, have you even talked to Aiden about all of this. About how he feels? Did you ever stop to consider that there are other ways to make him a father? You cannot just make this decision without discussing all the other options with him. You know as well as I do that if you ended up adopting one day, Aiden and his parents would love that baby just as fiercely as they would their own flesh and blood. Blood does not make a family. Love does." She stands up from the table. "Excuse me, I need to go to the restroom."

I watch as she walks away. She's pissed off and hurt. I wish I would have just kept my damn mouth shut. When she asked me what was really going on, I couldn't hold it in any longer. I just needed to release these feelings. Allison is my best friend; I need her. I'm startled from my thoughts when I hear the chair legs scrape across the floor.

Allison takes a sip of water and moves her salad around on her plate. She looks up and notices me watching her. She drops her fork. "Damn it, Hailey. You are crushing my heart right now. You have to know Aiden loves you, that he will always love you. You cannot make this decision. Please, just talk to him. Give him the chance to tell you how he feels about it," she pleads with me.

I can see how much this hurts her, so I agree. I won't do it though. I couldn't handle him telling me he agrees with what I'm saying. In my heart, I know the idea of Aiden speaking those words is ludicrous. However, my mind won't shut off. I see us ten years from now, he's miserable and saddled with a wife who he pledged to love till death do us part who cannot give him a family. I love him too much to let that happen. I need to set an end date. I need him to still be young enough to fall in love again and have time to have a family if I can't give him one.

Chapter Thirty-Three

L iam

After leaving the spa, Aiden and I hit the gym. It was nice to be there, just to be working out. No pressure of the team or upcoming games, just two friends lifting some weights. We lifted for a couple of hours. After hitting the showers, both our cells rang at the same time. Our wives have decided to end their day at a little café, and instruct us to pick them up in a couple of hours.

"Hey, let's head back to my place and throw a couple steaks on the grill. That should make it just about the right time to go pick them up," Aiden suggests.

Steak? I'm in. Especially after the workout we just put in. Not to mention, I ran five miles on the treadmill this morning. "Let's do it."

Aiden gets the steaks going while I grab a couple beers from the fridge. We settle out on the deck, enjoying the day. It's a warm day for May.

"Thanks for today, man, for suggesting the spa day for the girls. I hope Hales is able to relax. She's really stressing over not being able to get pregnant," Aiden tells me.

I hold my beer up in the air in recognition. "Hales has always been somewhat of a worrier. Look at how long she fought her attraction to you. She had herself convinced it would never work out and in the long run it would ruin not only the friendship you two had, but mine and yours as well."

"Yeah, I just wish she would talk to me. I can see it bothers her and she will admit that much, but there something else. Something she's not saying."

"Hales is a thinker. She lets her mind lead her when she should listen to her heart. You just have to give her some time," he says.

"I can do that. I can, but she's so distant. I want my wife back. We had married bliss for the first month or so, but now it's all about getting pregnant. Hell, if I would have known this is how it would turn out, I would have said we needed to wait, but just 'forgot' the condom. I want kids, but I want her more. I hate to see her stress over this, when it will happen. We have time, and if it doesn't, it doesn't."

I study him. "You mean that, don't you?" I ask.

"Seriously? You're going to ask me that. Of course I mean it. There is nothing in this world that means more to me than her. There are other ways for us to become parents. If she's not okay with that, we won't do it. I just want her happy. I want to see the sparkle in her eyes again. I want to feel like I'm connecting with her when we make love. Lately, it seems like it's just so I can fill her as she crosses her fingers, hoping my swimmers make it."

I don't say anything else about it and neither does he. We both know my sister needs time to work through whatever is going on in that head of hers. Aiden is just going to have to be patient. I can see it's tearing him up inside. Maybe girls' day helped.

"Steaks are ready," Aiden says a few minutes later. I hadn't even realized he left the table. We scarf them down like we haven't eaten in months. It's only been a few hours, but weight training builds an appetite.

Aiden pulls his cell phone out of his pocket and swipes the screen.

"We still have about an hour or so before going to pick them up. You up for some Call of Duty?" he asks.

"I'm game. It's been a while since I've kicked your ass on the Xbox," I chide him.

"Bring it, MacCoy," he fires back.

We battle it out for the next hour or so before leaving to pick up the girls.

I pull into the lot of the café and turn off my truck. Aiden pulls in right beside me. We make our way to the front entrance and see the girls are paying for their meals. Perfect timing. It's not until they turn to face us that I see something is not right.

Allison smiles softly as she walks toward me. She leans up on her tiptoes and kissed my cheek. "Thanks for today," she whispers.

Wrapping my arms around her waist, I pull hear against me and bury my face in her neck. I missed her. Yes, it's only been a few hours, but I missed her all the same. "Everything okay?" I say, my voice so low that only she can hear.

"I hope so. I'll fill you in later," she tells me. She pulls back and our eyes lock. "It's not me, Liam. The baby and I are fine. Hales is just dealing with some things and my heart aches for her," she tells me.

I instantly relax. I'm sure her conversation with Hales was similar to mine with Aiden. "Let's get you home, beautiful."

She doesn't respond. Instead, she laces her fingers through mine and leads me out to the truck. She didn't say hello to Aiden or goodbye to either one of them. What the fuck happened today?

I help Allison into the truck and wave to Aiden and Hales as we pull out of the lot. I reach over the console for Allison's hand. I missed my girl today. Once I make contact, I feel her shaking. I immediately pull over on the side of the road and put the truck in park. I turn to face her, bringing her hand to my lips. "Allie, baby, what's wrong? What happened today?" I ask.

I watch as a single tear slides down her cheek. My chest constricts from seeing her so upset. I hate it. It's not good for her or the baby. I catch the tear with my thumb. Her eyes find mine and I see so much sadness.

"Hales," she breathes out, "she wants a baby so bad. I'm just really worried about her," she tells me.

"I know, baby. Aiden said the same thing. He said she has been distant. I was kind of hoping that a girls' day might cheer her up," I say. I'm hoping my comment will pull more information out of her.

"We had a great day. It was nice to spend some time with just the two of us. Then we went for dinner and Hales..." she trails off shaking her head. "She's just so damn stubborn. I worry about her."

I lean over and kiss her temple. "Me too, baby. You know as well as I do, Hales has to work this out on her own."

Allison turns her head so we are face to face. "I just hope it's not too late," she whispers.

What? "Not too late for what?" I ask. I'm confused and she knows it.

"I'm just...I'm afraid if she can't get pregnant or if she doesn't soon, she will do something crazy like leave Aiden. She made a comment of how she hates the thought of not being able to make him a father," she explains.

"That's fucking crazy and you know it," I reply.

"I know. I just hope I'm wrong." Allison laces her fingers through mine. "I'm just ready to be home so I can curl up with you for a while."

This is her way of telling me she's not going to give me any more information. I'll just have to wait it out, but curling up with my wife sounds amazing right now.

Chapter Thirty-Four

iden

I was expecting to pick up my wife and find her glowing and happy from a day of pampering. What I found was two best friends with obvious tension between them. I had high hopes for today. I glance over at Hales who is sitting with her head back against the seat, staring out the window.

I reach over and place my hand on her thigh. "Did you enjoy your day, angel?" I need her to talk to me. I know if I try to pry, she will close up even more. I have to be patient and see if she will tell me on her own.

Without even glancing in my direction, she replies, "Yeah, it was nice. Thank you."

Now I know something's not right. Hales usually gushes about girls' day. She loves the spa and spending time with Allison. The two together usually have her chattering a mile a minute.

I'm too caught up in my own head to bother with a reply. Hailey doesn't seem to notice.

The fifteen minute drive feels like fifteen hours. I hate how she is so close, yet seems so far away. I don't know how to make her see it's her. She is all I want. Anything above that is just a bonus.

I follow her into the house and watch as she goes to the fridge and pulls out a bottle of water. She opens it and takes a long drink. Not able to stay away from her any longer, I walk up to her and take the bottle of water from her hands and sit it on the island. I then pick her up and sit her right beside it. Her legs fall open, allowing me to stand between them. I reach up and tuck a few stray strands of hair behind her ear. "I missed you today, angel."

Leaning down, I trail kisses down her neck, nipping and sucking as I go. I need to make love to her. I need to feel we still have that connection that is so deep it penetrates my soul. If we make a baby then great, perfect, but I just need to feel her, feel us.

I feel Hales place her hands on my chest and gently push. Standing up, I watch her as she pushes again. "I'm really tired, Aiden. It's been a long day. I think I'm just going to go to bed."

Her words catch me off guard. "It's only six o'clock," is my response. I'm shocked as hell. Who goes to bed at six o'clock?

"I know, but it was a long day. I could use a good night's sleep." She hops off the counter, stands on her tiptoes, and places a chaste kiss on my lips. "Goodnight. I love you," she says, her voice barely above a whisper.

I watch her as she walks away. My mind is reeling as to what the hell happened today. She's even more distant than before. Reaching into my pocket, I pull out my cell and hit Allison's number.

After three rings, I hear Liam's voice. "Hello?"

"Where's Allie? I need to talk to her." I don't bother with pleasantries. My world feels like it spinning out of control. My wife...I just need answers.

"She's in the shower. What's wrong?"

"What the fuck happened today? Hales is more distant than ever. She just went upstairs to go to bed. It's fucking six o'clock."

Liam releases a heavy sigh. "I'm not sure, man. Allison is upset too. She's not talking. The only thing I can get out of her is her heart hurts for Hales. She said Hailey wants a baby so bad and she feels guilty about our little peanut." Liam takes a deep breath. "My fucking wife is a mess and now you're telling me my sister is just as bad. No more fucking spa days," he says.

"Are they fighting?" I ask, my voice hesitant. I'm afraid of the answer. I've never known those two to fight. They have been thick as thieves from the day they met.

"No, I don't think so. Allie just seems sad for her and Hales just seems sad. I'll try to see if I can get anything else out of her, but I doubt she'll talk."

Fuck me. If Allie doesn't tell Liam, I know I won't be able to get it out of her. "Okay. Just call me if you find anything out."

I hit end and throw my phone down. I brace both hands against the counter and bow my head. How did things go from bad to worse so fast? I just need her to talk to me. Deciding that I'm not going to let her push me away, I head to bed. I don't care that I won't be able to sleep; I just need to be near her. I just need to fix this.

I gently push open our bedroom door and see her lying on her side of the bed. She's facing the other way, so I can't see her face. I strip out of my clothes and throw them in the hamper. I know it drives her crazy when I leave them lay. The last thing I need to do is give her more reason to pull away from me.

I lift up the covers and slide into bed. I don't stop in my side; instead, I slide as close to her as I can get and wrap my arms around her. I can tell by her breathing that she's not asleep. Instead of trying to talk, I decide I just want to hold her. I place a soft kiss on her shoulder. "I love you, angel," I whisper against her ear.

I feel her body shake and I know she's crying. I don't ask her to talk. I don't ask what I can do. I pull her tighter against my chest and hope she can feel the love I have for her. Watching her like this is killing me. I silently will her to open up to me as we lay here in the darkness. I tell her again how much I love her as sleep claims me.

Chapter Thirty-Five

llison

We haven't seen much of Hailey and Aiden these past few weeks. We still get together once a week for dinner, but it used to be three or four times per week. That has pretty much stopped. The guys had to fly to Los Angeles for some promo commercials for the team. Training camp starts in two weeks and this is something a few players from each team have to take part in. They left yesterday and will not be back until the day after tomorrow. Liam called Hailey, his mom, and Aiden's mom to make sure they all check on me while he is gone. He still says he feels like something is going to happen and he's not going to be here. I can see the true concern in his eyes, so I don't bother fighting with him over it. If it makes him feel better, I'm good with it. Besides, I love my mother-in-law, and Aiden's mom has been my surrogate mother for years. I love those two and any time we get to spend together is precious.

Today is Hailey's day and I smile as I look at the clock and see it's almost noon. She should be here any minute. She called first thing to check on me. I assured her I am perfectly fine. She suggested she wait until noon to stop by and she would bring lunch. I've been craving the little pizza place in town, so she's going to stop there and pick up lunch. My best friend/sister-in-law is amazing.

I am currently sitting on the couch with my feet propped up. I've had a little bit of swelling. The doctor said not to be concerned last week at my visit. He just advised me to take it easy and prop my feet up whenever I could. So here I am all propped up, my Kindle in hand, and my cell within reach. Soon I will have my best friend and yummy pizza to join the mix. What more could a girl ask for?

I hear keys in the door. "Allie," Hailey calls out. Her voice sounds a little off.

"In here," I call back.

Hailey comes around the corner carrying a pizza box, paper plates, napkins, and two bottles of water.

"Ask and you shall receive," she says with a smile that doesn't reach her eyes.

I wait until we are both served and perched on the couch before I address her lack of good mood. She's usually better at hiding it. She's barely touched her food and now that I really look, I can see her eyes are a little puffy.

I set my plate on the table and turn to face her. I reach over and grab her free hand. She follows my lead and sets her plate on the end table. "Hailey, what's wrong?" No point in beating around the bush.

Biting down on her lip, she shakes her head no. I watch as tears leak from her eyes like a faucet. I have no idea what could have caused this reaction out of her. "Hales, you're scaring me. Please tell me what happened?" I'm pleading with her. Instead of her getting angry like I assumed she would, she reaches over and grabs her phone. She swipes the screen a few times before handing it to me, her hands shaking.

I take the phone from her and take a deep breath before peering down at the screen. It's a grainy picture of Aiden sitting across from a woman at a restaurant. The setting appears to be intimate, but it's hard to really tell. I search for Liam in the picture, but there is no sight of him. "Hailey, you know the press blows things out of proportion. You need to call him and ask him about this," I say.

"No, no way. I can't hear him tell me that he's with someone else. I can't do it, Allison," she cries.

"Hales, listen to me. Aiden loves you. Only you. This picture is being taken out of context, I can assure you. Do you think Liam would let this happen? You're his baby sister." I'm getting frustrated with her. I know she's heartbroken. I can honestly say I would be thrown off as well, but being the wives of famous League players, we have to get used to tabloids telling stories that are in no way true about our lives. Hailey knows this.

"What other excuse could there be? It's obvious they are on a date."

"No, it's really not obvious," I argue. The picture does look incriminating, but I know Aiden would never do that. Hailey is it for him. I know things have been rocky for them these past few months, but he would never. If Hailey was not so down on herself for not being able to get pregnant, she could open her eyes and see Aiden would never do this to her.

"Looks like I won't have to worry about how I'm going to leave him; he's taking care of that all on his own." She wipes the tears from her cheeks.

Gripping both of her hands tightly, I try to reason with her. "Hailey, listen to what you're saying. This is Aiden, your husband. Remember the man you fought for. You went through so much to be together. Do you really think he would just throw that all away without a second thought?" I ask.

"I just...I don't know anymore. I can't help but push him away, thinking in the long run he will be better off. Then I see this picture and I'm completely heartbroken. That man," she points to her phone, "he is my heart. I want so much to give him a family. To bring him an ounce of the happiness that he has given me. I'm a fucking failure at being a wife." She cries harder.

I move so I am sitting as close to her as possible with my protruding belly and put my arms around her, trying to give her the comfort she needs. I know she needs him. I say a silent prayer that the two of them can work this out.

Chapter Thirty-Six

H ailey

I feel Allison wrap her arms around my shoulders and that only makes me cry harder. Now that the tears have started, I can't seem to stop them. My heart tells me that Aiden would never, but that picture... I just want him back, my Aiden. I want to be happy and carefree. I know the reason we aren't is because of me, but I just can't get past the fact that I can't give him what he wants.

Allison holds me and just lets me cry. I let it all out. The last few months have been so stressful. Not only have I worried about getting pregnant, but the distance between me and Aiden is like a knife to my heart. On top of that, we have been spending less time with Allison and Liam. I fought with her and that's when the distance started. I broke my promise to Allison. I told her I would talk about this with Aiden, but I didn't. I couldn't. I'm too scared.

"Hales," she says my name like she's afraid I will go into full mental breakdown any minute. I guess with the way I have been all over with my emotions the last few months, I can see how she would feel that way.

"I'm going to call Liam." I tense at her words. "I'm not going to mention the picture. I just want to see what they are up to, what they did last night. Maybe he can give us more information without us directly asking him. Have you talked to Aiden?"

I sit up so she can get in a more comfortable position. I lift her legs back onto the coffee table. "No, he called last night after I was asleep. I didn't hear my phone. He tried again, but I had just seen the picture and I didn't answer."

Allison nods in understanding. She grabs her phone and dials Liam. He picks up immediately and I can hear from the sound of his voice that he's happy to hear from her. Aiden used to be that way. Things have been so strained between us lately that I can't remember the last time either one of us was truly that happy. Regret washes over me; I did this to us.

The ringing of my cell phone startles me. I look down to see my husband's smiling face. With shaking hands, I swipe the screen and answer. "Hello?"

"It's good to hear your voice, angel," he replies. "I missed talking to you last night and again this morning. I was starting to worry. Then I heard Liam say you were at his house with Allie, so I thought I would try my luck again. Looks like third times a charm." He laughs, but I can tell it's forced.

"So how's the shoot?" I'm trying hard not to ask him about the picture. I don't want to interfere with what he's doing for the team.

"Good. Long days. Liam and I went out to dinner last night with John." He's quiet for a minute before he says, "I miss you, baby," his voice gruff.

"Me too," I reply. I do, I miss him like crazy, not just physically, but emotionally. Something has to happen, neither one of us can keep living this way. I need to just do what Allison told me to do all those weeks ago and talk to him. Lay it all out on the table and let the cards fall where they may. However, their agent John was nowhere in the picture, neither was Liam. I know my brother would not let this happen without words and a few fists being thrown. GAH. My head is a jumbled fucking mess right now.

"Hales, when I get home..." his voice is shaky, "when I come home to you, I need us to talk about this, the distance between us. I fucking hate it. I hate feeling like I'm losing you each day."

I can hear the emotion in his voice. I can hear the sincerity. "Yeah, we need to talk. We'll talk when you get back," I say, trying to keep my voice as steady as possible.

"Not when I get back. When I come home, to you. You're my home, Hales."

Those words have the river of tears once again flowing rapidly over my cheeks. I suck in deep even breaths to try to gain control before I speak again. He waits quietly on the other line. I can hear him breathing. "I love you, Aiden. We'll talk, I promise." I vow to do just that. I know I have been shutting him out, pushing him away. We do need to let it all out and then decide how we move forward. I refuse to ask him about the girl until we are face to face. There is an ache deep in my chest at the thought that in just a few days my marriage could be over.

After a couple of "talk to you soon" and another round of "I love you," Allison and I both are off the phone.

"Did you ask him?" she questions me immediately.

"No, I want to do it in person. I don't want to interfere with the work they are doing out there. He did say we needed to talk and I agree." I mess with the hem of my shorts. "I never talked to him," I confess.

"I know."

I turn to face her. "What do you mean, you know? How would you know?"

Allison smiles. "Hailey Emerson, that man loves you with fierce determination. There is no way in hell you talked to him about your worries and the distance still be there. Trust me on this one."

I watch as she picks up her plate of cold pizza and begins to eat. I do the same, even though my stomach is in knots. Two days until he comes home. Two days until I come clean with the man I love and wait for him to leave me.

Chapter Thirty-Seven

L iam

Aiden and I are sharing a room. It feels like college again. We decide to order in and just relax. Allie sounded good earlier. She promised me she was feeling great and staying off her feet as much as possible just like the doctor ordered. Yesterday was Mom's day to spend with her. She said Allie looks as beautiful as ever. There is no doubt that my girl is beautiful. Pregnancy definitely agrees with her. Her belly is growing and I can't keep my hands off her. I talk to our baby every day. I want him or her to know me, to know I love them already. We decided we are going to find out what we are having so we can pick out a name and get the nursery ready.

"Shit. I was supposed to tell you Allison says hi," I relay the message to Aiden. I forgot to tell him when I talked to Allison earlier.

He smiles. "How is she?"

"Good. Hales is there with her today, but I'm sure you know that." I grab another slice of pizza out of the box. "How's Hales? I saw you take a call when I was talking to Allison earlier at the shoot." I know they are going through a rough patch. My sister needs to get her head out of her ass. I'm ready to tell her just that. My wife is upset and that is not good for her or our baby.

"Different this time. She was really quiet. I told her that when I get home, we have to talk. I need to know what's going on in that head of hers that's causing her to push me away."

"I agree, man. Even if you have to tie her ass down, she needs to let you in. You are her husband. I should have warned you before you married her," I joke.

"Nothing would have stopped me from marrying her. Nothing. I will fight for her, with her, for her, until the day I die," he says through gritted teeth.

I hold my hands up in surrender. "I didn't mean to piss you off. Hales just has a habit of getting into her own head and her damn stubbornness sometimes prevents her from seeing what's right in front of her. I love my sister, but I hate how she's acting," I defend myself. The last thing I need is for us to come to blows.

I make my way to the mini fridge and grab us both another beer. "A peace offering." I smirk.

"Sorry, man. She and I just need to hammer this out."

"Why don't you take her away for the weekend? Maybe book a suite and lock her inside until you get it worked out. Maybe a change of scenery, a romantic one, will help." I shrug. I'm not really good at this unless it's for Allie. I know what makes my wife smile.

"You know, that's not a bad idea." He grabs his phone, and within minutes, he has a luxury suite at the Ritz Carlton reserved for three nights. "I went ahead and booked it for tomorrow night too. I thought maybe if we finish early enough tomorrow, we could try to change our flight home?"

"Let's see, get home to my wife sooner than expected? Hell yeah, I'm in. Actually, they said we would only be needed if there are re-shoots." I pull out my phone and call John, our agent. "Hey, John, it's Liam. Have you heard if we're needed for the re-shoots tomorrow?" I stand to pace the room. Now that the idea is there, I will do whatever it takes to make it happen.

"Actually, they just called. You and Aiden are both good to go. I was just getting ready to call you and let you know," he tells me.

"Awesome. Thanks, man. We are going to try to change our flights and fly home early."

John laughs. "Sounds good. Tell Allison and Hailey I said hello." Our agent knows us so well.

"Will do," I say and hit the end key. I immediately dial the airline and see about getting our flights changed. "They can get us on the red-eye direct flight. We would be back in Charlotte around five."

"Do it," is his reply.

"We have a couple of hours before we have to leave. Aiden looks at his watch. It's ten in Charlotte. You think we should call them and tell them we're coming home early?"

"No, I want to take Hales by surprise. The grand gesture. I want to swoop in and whisk her off to the hotel," Aiden says. I can see the wheels turning in his head.

"Sounds good. I'm always up for surprising my girl," I tell him.

We finish eating and watch some ESPN before we check out of the hotel and head to the airport. I can't wait to get home, slide into bed next to her, and place my hand on her belly and fall asleep with her in my arms. The excitement of going home early is going to keep me wide-awake on the plane.

Chapter Thirty-Eight

iden

Neither one of us slept on the plane. We are both hyped to be home to our wives a day early. I've ran a million different scenarios through my mind. Things that I want to say to my wife. It all boils down to her. Did she really mean what she said on the phone? Is she finally willing to let me know what's going on in the beautiful head of hers? Will she willingly come with me to the hotel I reserved? My mind won't stop racing.

After leaving the airport, I drop Liam off at his place and head home to Hailey. I don't bother parking in the garage. I don't want the door to wake her, and I hope that as soon as she can throw a few things in an overnight bag, we will be heading to the hotel. I hope I can convince her.

As quietly as possible, I place my key in the door and turn the lock. The house is quiet with shimmers of the morning sunrise casting a glow through the windows. Locking the door back, I kick off my shoes and softly climb the stairs. Our bedroom door is open. Hailey is laying on my side of the bed clutching my pillow close to her chest. I get a warm feeling deep in my gut at the sight. She misses me, which is a good sign. I strip out of my clothes and climb into her side of the bed. This is not the original plan, but I cannot pass up holding a sleeping Hailey in my arms. Never gonna happen.

I slide in behind her and place my arms around her. She moans my name and burrows deeper into my embrace. Just that small act has me wanting to cry like a fucking baby. It's been weeks since she's wanted to be close to me. Hell, we've only made love twice since her spa day. Each time, I could tell she was distracted.

Hailey rolls over so we are chest to chest, face to face. I gently tuck several loose tendrils of hair behind her ear. Her eyes flutter open and those baby blues I love are staring back at me. "Morning, angel." I keep my voice low.

She blinks a few times. I can tell she's confused, so I explain. "We finished a day early. We took the red-eye home. I didn't want to waste another day there when I could be here with you."

Hailey places her hand on my cheek. "You look tired." My heart is thundering in my chest. This is another good sign. I've missed this. Just being with her, being close to her.

"Baby, can you go somewhere with me?" I can see the question in her eyes as soon as my words register. "I have a surprise for you. I need for you to pack a bag for a few days. Can you do that? We need time away from the familiar and that includes our home, so we can talk about us. Talk about what's been keeping you away from me." My voice is pleading.

"When do we leave?" she asks.

I release the breath I'm holding. "As soon as you're ready. I thought we could stop at the bakery you love and pick up some breakfast. We're not going far," I explain.

She doesn't answer me with words. Instead, she rolls out of bed and begins to throw a few items of clothing into her overnight bag. Mine is still in the car, so I'm good. I watch as she steps into the bathroom and returns with her toothbrush and a few other necessities and places them in her bag. She grabs her cell phone from the nightstand and slides her feet into a pair of flip-flops. She then turns to look at me. "Ready," she says softly. She's still being distant. I hope we can work through this.

I miss my wife.

I reach for her bag with one hand, and her hand with the other. I give it a gentle squeeze as I lead her down the stairs. I open the front door and make sure it's locked tight. Hailey is already in the car by the time I'm done. I pop the trunk and toss her luggage in with mine. Please let this work, let me convince her to open up to me.

I drive to the bakery she loves. Leaning over the seat, I kiss her cheek. "I'll be right back. You want your usual?" I ask, even though I know the answer.

"Yes, thank you."

It takes me no time at all to order her apple turnover that she loves. She also likes the banana nut muffins. I order two of each. I grab two cherry turnovers and two chocolate chip muffins for me. I'm sure the Ritz has good snack food, but I just want this to be perfect. I add two large coffees to the order and head back to the car. Hailey's eyes go wide at the size of the bag. She doesn't comment.

It's only a ten-minute drive from the bakery to the Ritz.

"Wow," she breathes when we pull up to the valet parking.

I toss my keys to the valet after grabbing our bags from the trunk. Hailey has all of our goodies from the bakery. I step to the reception desk and give them my name. I checked in over the phone for privacy purposes. The guy at the desk slides two cards across the counter. He remains professional, never asking for an autograph. I can tell he knows who I am, but he stays in professional mode and doesn't ask. I make a mental note to sign one for him when we check out. Right now, I need to get my wife up to that room.

The room is huge with a king size bed, kitchenette, and living room area. The bathroom is huge with a stand-up shower big enough for several people and a huge garden tub. Hailey places our breakfast in the kitchen area while I kick off my shoes and set our bags in the walk-in closet. This is like a small apartment.

Hailey, who is still wearing her shorts and tank she slept in, removes her bra, and climbs into bed. I watch her, waiting for her to ask me to join her. No way am I letting her get away with pushing me away anymore. I've stood by without fighting long enough. "I know you're exhausted. I can see it in your eyes. Let's sleep for a few more hours and then we can have breakfast."

That's what I was waiting for. She invited me into bed with her. I strip down to my boxer briefs and crawl under the covers. I reach out for her and she comes to me willingly. She rests he head on my chest while I gently stroke her back. I feel her body relax against me. "Love you," I say as I drift off to sleep.

Chapter Thirty-Nine

A llison

I've been tossing and turning all night. My little baby bump prevents me from sleeping on my belly. That's how I always sleep unless Liam is here. Then I sleep either on his chest or on my side with him behind me, always in his arms. I miss my husband. One more night and he'll be home.

Just as I'm about to give up on sleep all together, I hear the front door open and close. At first, I freeze in fear. I jump out of bed and go to the window to see Aiden's car sitting in the drive. He's home early. I'm sure he wanted it to be a surprise, so I run back to bed and try to calm my racing heart. I hear his pants hit the floor, and feel the bed dip and warm arms around me. I've calmed enough that he doesn't realize I'm awake. He kisses my shoulder and gently tugs so I'm lying on my back. I feel him slide his t-shirt up over my baby bump. Just as quick, his lips are against my skin, kissing our baby.

Liam rubs my belly affectionately. I can feel his hot breath against my skin. "Hey, kiddo. Daddy missed you and Mommy. I missed you so much I flew through the night. I hope you've been good in there? Taking it easy on your momma. She needs to rest." He places another kiss on my expanding belly. "I love you, kiddo."

I try to stop the tears, but it just isn't possible. I never would have thought that it would be possible to fall further in love with Liam, but I do in this moment. I lift my hand to wipe my tears, which catches his attention.

He pulls himself up on top of me and his lips meet mine. I savor the taste of him. All too soon he pulls away and settles in beside me. He props himself up on his elbow. "Why the tears, baby?" he asks. I can hear the concern in his voice.

"These are happy tears, you goof. I heard everything you said when you were talking to the baby. I just fell in love with you all over again."

"I love you more every day. Both of you," he says, rubbing my baby bump.

He then tells me how they wrapped up early and decided to fly home last night. He proceeds to tell me all about the shoot and Aiden's plans to kidnap Hailey and get her to talk to him. I don't mention the picture. I'll wait until Aiden and Hales work though that particular issue before mentioning it to Liam.

"Allie, you look exhausted. I thought you were taking it easy?"

"I can't sleep. I sleep on my belly when you're not here and, well, this is the first time you've been away since the peanut started growing."

Liam slides down and pulls me against his chest. "Let's sleep. I was prepared to stay up to spend time with you. I didn't fly all night just to sleep, but turns out we both win." He kisses the top of my head. "I get you in my arms and we both get sleep," he says with a yawn.

I wake to the sun shining bright. I'm in the same exact spot I was when we fell asleep, on his chest with his arms around me. I peek up at him and see he is still sound asleep. I glance at the clock on the night-stand and it says it's after three. We slept all day. I needed it, and so did he. I was not looking forward to another night without him. I don't know what I'm going to do when training camp starts next week. I've read that a lot of women end up sleeping in recliners during pregnancy due to back pain and not being able to get comfortable. Sadness hits me as I wish my mom was here so I could ask her these questions.

I gently slide out of bed and rush to the bathroom. I can't believe I slept as long as I did without having to go to the bathroom. It's a nightly ritual these days. I quietly slip out of the bedroom and downstairs to get a glass of orange juice. I'm startled to find Aiden's and Liam's moms in our kitchen drinking coffee. Then it hits me that Mrs. Emerson was supposed to be the one to sit with me today.

"Good morning," they say in unison.

"Good morning. I'm sorry I didn't call you. Liam and Aiden finished a day early, so they flew home last night. I haven't been sleeping well, so when Liam climbed into bed and I curled up against him, we were pretty much out for count," I rush to explain.

"No problem, honey. At first, I was worried, so I called in reinforcements," she says, pointing to Liam's mom. "I knew she had a key. As soon as we unlocked the door, we saw his luggage and shoes."

"We assumed you would wake soon, so we made breakfast and a pot of coffee. Are you hungry?" she asks.

"Starving," I hear his deep voice rumble behind me. I then feel his arms around my waist and his hand caress my belly. "Afternoon, beautiful," he says, not caring who hears him. He kisses my cheek and guides me to the table, pulling out a chair for me. He waits for me to sit, and then kisses the top of my head. He makes his way around the table, kissing both his mom and Aiden's on the cheek. I watch as he makes two plates of biscuits and gravy with strips of bacon and places them in the microwave. A few minutes later, I have a piping hot plate of food and a tall glass of OJ in front of me.

As I sit and take it all in, I am filled with love and happiness. You might think it's weird that I'm not upset to find the mothers in my kitchen, not know they were there, but I'm not. I love them both. I love having family who care, who rush to make sure I'm okay. People who I know I can depend on. I embrace it with open arms.

Chapter Forty

H^{ailey}

I wake up lying on Aiden's chest. I stay as still as I can, just listening to his heartbeat. I gently lift up to look at him and find him awake. He offers me a sad smile. I know I can't put this off any longer. Needing just a few more minutes, I climb out of bed and go to the restroom. I take care of business before brushing my teeth. I take my time and realize it's not going to prevent the conversation that I know we need to have.

I find Aiden sitting up in bed, staring out the window. We forgot to close them early this morning when we checked in. Not that it matters; we are on the fifteenth floor. Don't have to worry about photographers and peeping Toms when you're up this high.

I climb back into bed and sit Indian style facing my husband. I take a deep breath and slowly exhale. Then the words come spilling out of me.

"First, I need you to tell me who's in this picture." I hand him my cell phone, which I picked up off the dresser on my way back from the bathroom.

He takes my phone and glances at the picture. "That's Lisa, John's wife." He hands my phone back to me. Then it hits him. "Wait, did you think...?" He leans forward and cups my cheek with his hands. "Baby, there is no one in this world for me but you. Don't ever doubt your importance in my life. Liam and I had dinner with John and Lisa. Liam went to the restroom and John stepped out of the noisy restaurant to take a call. Nothing more, nothing less. Hailey, you're my wife. I would never..." His voice cracks.

"I know," I say, defeated. "My heart knows, but when I saw the picture and I've already been feeling inadequate as a wife, I let my imagination run wild. Allison tried to tell me it was just the tabloids trying to earn a buck, but I just kept thinking about you with her."

Aiden puts his hands on my waist and lifts me into his lap, holding me against his chest. "Baby, why did you say that? What makes you think you are inadequate as my wife? Have I done something? Said something to make you feel that way?" His voice is laced with hurt.

I'm glad I am no longer looking at him. Maybe I will be able to keep the tears at bay for the next part of this conversation. "No. You didn't do or say anything, but I can't give you babies. I know you want to be a father, and I can't do that for you. As your wife, I am supposed to carry your ba-babies." I break off in a sob.

His arms tighten around me so tight that I can barely breathe. I don't say anything and I don't try to move from his embrace. I need this. I need to feel his arms around me. I need to soak up every single second of time like this with him while I can.

When my sobs quiet, he relaxes his hold a little. In a voice filled with emotion, he asks, "Hailey, can you please switch positions so I can see your face? I need to see you." His voice is sad, pleading.

I lift up to move, and the next thing I know, he has me straddling his hips. His back is still resting against the headboard and we are face to face. He keeps one hand in a tight grip on my hip; the other, he traces the outline of my jaw. "Please, look at me."

I've been staring at his chest, not wanting to make eye contact, not wanting to hear what he says next. Swallowing back the lump in my throat, I allow my eyes to meet his. I didn't expect them to be filled with tears, but they are.

"Hailey, how do I make you understand that you are the most important person in the world to me? How can I show you that my heart, my soul, belongs to you? How can I prove to you that my life without you is not worth living? We fought hard to get here, Hales. We battled our inner demons and what we thought others would think and feel. I lost so much fucking time with you. I don't want to lose another second. Do I want to be a father? Yes, I want kids. Do I want to do it without you? No, I don't. Hailey, what you don't understand is that when I picture me as a father, you are there right beside me. I don't want that without you. If we keep trying and the end result is that we— not you Hales—we cannot get pregnant, we can adopt. If you don't want to adopt, we will just spoil Liam and Allie's kids rotten and then send them home. Baby, it's all nothing without you. Those dreams of my future are entwined with you. If you are not a part of my life, neither are those dreams." He stops to study me, giving me time to process what he's saying.

I can feel the tears running unchecked down my face. His eyes are glassy, but no tears have fallen. I debate on whether or not I should tell him that I was prepared to let him go. I know if we are truly going to move past this, I need to. "I was going to let you go. Push you away so you had enough of me. I wanted you to find someone to love who would give you babies. Someone who could make your dreams come true." I rush the words so I can't change my mind.

"Hailey, I will never love another woman. Never. No one will ever replace you. You own me. My dreams, all of them, revolve around you, not just starting a family. My career, retirement, and every aspect of my life is centered around you and the love I have for you." He leans in and rests his forehead against mine. "Baby, I need you to tell me you under-stand that. I need to know you're not leaving me," he begs.

"I...are you sure?" My heart is screaming at me to shut the hell up. While in the back of my mind, I still worry I will be keeping him from living out one of his dreams.

"Hailey Emerson, I cannot live without you. I want it all, but only with you. Whatever life throws our way."

"You're okay with adoption?" I ask, needing reassurance.

"Hell yes. Blood does not make you family. If we are told we cannot conceive traditionally, then I would want nothing more than to adopt a child we can love and nurture. Everything, angel. As long as you are by my side. We're a team, Mrs. Emerson," he whispers.

I'm an idiot. I let my insecurities jeopardize my marriage. I hold his face with both hands, wanting to look right at him when I say this. "Aiden, I am so sorry for letting my doubts and insecurities into our marriage. I'm sorry I didn't trust our love enough to know we would work through it. I'm so sorry. Please, can you forgive me? I love you. My heart aches for you. I've been miserable and I know it's my fault. I just..." My words trail off as I see a single tear slide down his cheek. I watch as it reaches my thumb and I gently wipe it away.

"Nothing to be sorry for, angel. Just remember you need to talk to me. We can always work it out, but you have to be honest with me. Fuck, Hales, I could have lost you." His voice cracks.

I need to show him. I need to prove that I'm here and love him with everything in me. We have not had sex in weeks, and when we did, it was mechanical. All my fault. I need to change that, starting now.

Chapter Forty-One

L iam

Allison and I are just lounging around today. Mine and Aiden's mom left after we finished eating. Now we are on the couch. I have my back propped up against the arm, and Allison is lying between my legs. She's reading her Kindle while I watch ESPN. In one hand I have the remote; the other I have resting on Allie's baby bump. I cherish days like today. Next week, Aiden and I will be leaving for training camp. I hate I'm going to miss so much of the pregnancy. I still have this nagging feeling that I need to be by her side at all times. I guess being irrational runs in our family.

I'm skimming through the channels, asking Allie what she wants to do for dinner, when I feel a thump against my hand. The hand that's on my wife's stomach. "What the hell was that?" I ask Allison. I gently push her up and stand up. Something's wrong. I reach in my pocket for my phone and it's not there. "Allie, baby, everything is going to be fine. I'm just going to run into the kitchen to get the house phone and call the doctor. I want him to meet us at the hospital." My words are rushed. I'm fucking panicking. I run to the kitchen, grab the cordless phone and make a mad dash back to the living room. I find Allison standing in the middle of the room, her face lit up with joy. What. The. Hell?

"Liam, calm down. I'm fine; the baby is fine. What you felt was a kick," she says with a chuckle. "Our little peanut is becoming more active every day. He or she is finally kicking hard enough that you can feel it too. This is what's been going on inside of me the last couple of weeks."

I throw the phone on the couch and drop to my knees in front of her. I gently lift her shirt. She grabs the hem and holds it up for me. I need to see this happen again. I place both of my hands on her belly. I place my lips just above her belly button and place a kiss there. I move back slightly. "Hey, peanut, it's Daddy. I felt your kick against my hand. That's an awesome trick. Can you do it again for me?" Just as I open my mouth to ask Allie if the baby is moving, I not only feel the kick, but I see it. A tiny knot forms on her belly, and then it's gone in a flash. I look up to my wife for reassurance that she's okay.

"I'm fine, Daddy. The baby likes the sound of your voice. Earlier on the couch, it happened when you asked me about dinner. He or she knows who you are," she tells me. My heart is beating so fast; the baby can probably hear it. This is an experience I will never forget as long as I live.

"Does it hurt?"

Allison smiles at me. "Sometimes, but it's all worth it. There's not a whole lot of room in there."

I move my lips back next to her belly. "I love you, peanut. Take it easy on Mommy." Before I'm finished, it happens again. Tears prick the back of my eyes at the miracle that we created. Suddenly, I can't wait until the end of next month for another ultrasound.

Standing up, I lead Allie back to the couch and help her sit. I grab the house phone and dial her doctor's office. "Hi, this is Liam MacCoy; my wife, Allison, is a patient. I was wondering if you all can fit us in today for an ultrasound." I listen as the receptionist explains that our insurance will only cover so many unless there are complications. She then proceeds to tell me about a place called Becoming Mom. They offer pampering for expectant mothers. They also offer three dimensional ultrasounds. She also mentions they are rather expensive, so not many get them. I thank her for the information, hang up, and dial the number she gave me. Turns out this place is just across town and they can work us in, but we have to be there in forty minutes. It's about a thirty-minute drive, so I tell her to put us on the books.

"Ready to see our baby, beautiful girl? Come on, we have to hurry; it's across town. I will explain in the car," I tell her.

She laughs at me as I assist her off the couch. She slides her feet into her flip-flops and we are out the door.

As soon as we are in the car, I fill her in on my phone call with her doctor's office. I expect her to be excited about this, but when I glance at her, she's laughing again.

"Liam, I knew about this place already," she says.

"Then why in the hell haven't we done this already?" I ask her.

"You have a better chance of learning the sex the farther along you are."

"Wait, do you think they will be able to tell?" I'm excited as hell. Not only do I get to see our baby on the screen and see how he or she has grown, we might also get to quit calling he or she a peanut and pick out a name.

Allison throws her head back and laughs. "Yeah, babe. It's a possibility. I'm sixteen weeks, so depending if peanut here cooperates, we might be able to find out," she says.

"Is the ultrasound bad for the baby? Like x-rays?" I ask, concerned.

"Not at all; they are safe."

I bring our hands of entwined fingers to my lips and kiss her knuckles. "So that means we can do this as much as we want?"

She turns her head to look at me. "Liam, it's expensive. I'm not sure how expensive, but the average person doesn't do it because insurance doesn't cover it."

"Baby, you know as well as I do that the cost is not an issue. I think we should do it again the farther along we get. Maybe every few weeks," I tell her.

"Every few weeks?" she gasps.

"Okay, maybe once a month until we deliver," I relent.

Allison just shakes her head at me, a beautiful smile plastered across her face.

<h1>Chapter Forty-Two</h1>

 iden

My beautiful wife is straddling my hips, and it's been weeks since I've made love to her, since we've connected that way. My heart is about to pound out of my chest from our conversation. I can't believe she was going to push me away, leave me. Fuck. I can't even let myself think about my life without her in it. Never again will I let her silently stew to let her work through her feelings. I don't care if it causes us to argue every damn day. We will talk about it. I told her I would fight with her, for her, and because of her. I meant it.

I stand up with Hales still on my lap. She immediately clamps her legs around my waist and places her hands around my neck, holding on. I have the sudden need to shower; not only has it been a long night with the flight home, but I just feel like we need to cleanse it all away. This is a step forward in our marriage; an additional vow has been made.

I carry her into the bathroom and kick the door closed. I sit her down on the counter, but she keeps her legs clamped around me. Cupping her face with my hands, I lean in and kiss her. My tongue makes a pass over her bottom lip and that's all it takes for her to open for me. I slip inside and she meets me stroke for stroke. I'm hard as a rock, so I press my hips against her and she moans deep in her throat.

This, this passion. This is what we've missed the past couple of months. The connection. I should kick my own ass for letting her get inside her head like that and not forcing her to talk to me.

Grabbing the hem of her shirt, I begin to lift. Hailey, reading my mind, lifts her arms in the air, allowing me to undress her. I toss her shirt behind us. I quickly step out of my boxer briefs and lift her off the counter. I kneel before her and slide her boy shorts down, following the action with a trail of kisses. Hailey places her hands on my shoulders to brace herself in order to step out of them. Standing up, I pull her against me. Nothing between us, I bury my face in her neck and just breathe her in. I can feel my hands tremble as I gently stroke her back.

"Aiden?" her voice is soft and questioning.

Lifting my head, I seek out those blue eyes of hers. "Hales, I just… I'm so fucking sorry I didn't fight for us. I've missed you so much, baby," I choke out the words past the emotion clogging my throat. I see tears in her eyes. Needing to wash the sadness away, I lean in and turn the water on in the shower. After adjusting the temperature, I turn back to Hales and offer her my hand. She takes it and follows me into the hot spray.

I ache to be inside her, but I won't do it here. I'm not going to take her against the shower wall after weeks of being apart. We have the rest of the day and all day tomorrow for that. Right now, I want to wash every inch of our skin, and then take her to bed. I want to make love to her. I want that soul deep connection. I want to take my time with her. I need that.

Grabbing the shower gel, I lather up my hands and gently rub them across her skin. No part of her goes untouched. After washing her hair, she mimics my actions. I have to sit on the bench seat so she can wash my hair. She's standing between my legs. I've had about all the foreplay I can handle. Hailey seems to be reading my mind because we both make quick work of drying off. She doesn't even bother with her hair. She towel dries it and lets the wet tendrils fall down her back.

Swooping down, I cradle her in my arms and carry her to the bed. I lay her in the middle and climb on top of her. Reaching up, she places her hands behind my neck and pulls me down into a kiss. I dive in, nipping and sucking her lips, tasting her. Her legs fall open, allowing me to nestle against her heat. She wraps her legs around my waist and pulls me close. We both moan as I slip inside. I don't move, just relish the feel of her warmth wrapped around me.

Home.

I'm finally home. I spend the next hour showing her how much I love her. I make sure my strokes are gentle as I kiss and caress her.

"Aiden...more. I need..." she pants.

"No, angel. I want this slow. I want you to know how much I cherish you. I need you to remember this moment the next time you think about leaving me. I need you to remember this feeling." I push in hard as far as I can go and still. "I need you to engrave this in your mind. No one will ever mean to me what you do. No one can ever love you like I do."

I begin a steady, slow rhythm that I can feel is about to throw her over the edge. As soon as I feel her clench around me, I let loose. My thrusts are hard and fast, pushing us both over the edge.

I slip out and lay down beside her. I gather her in my arms and hold her as tight as I can without crushing her. I never want to let her go. Jesus, I leave for training camp next week. Can we make it through that? Will she begin to second guess us again?

"Hales, training camp is next week. Are we—" she stops me with a kiss.

"Yes, we are solid. I'm so sorry for putting us through this."

I breathe a sigh of relief at her words. We're solid. "I love you, Hailey Emerson," I say before showing her just how much.

Chapter Forty-Three

llison

As we pull into the parking lot of Becoming Mom, I can't keep the goofy grin off my face. Liam and I are about to see our baby, and maybe find out what we're having. Liam is so excited. He's going to be the best father.

He walks us straight to the counter and signs in. We are immediately taken back to a room. The tech hands me a gown and says I can keep my pants on, just unbutton them. Um...I'm wearing yoga pants. I assume that's her common spiel she tells all of her patients. I make my way into the small bathroom, which is attached to the exam room, to change into the gown. I can hear Liam's heavy footsteps pacing the floor the entire time.

After changing, Liam helps me get settled on the exam table, and then resumes his pacing.

"Liam," I scold him.

He stops to face me. "I'm sorry. I'm so fucking excited about this." He walks to me and takes the chair next to the table. "After feeling our peanut, it's just all the more real. I mean, I know we've seen early pictures and we hear the heartbeat every month, but feeling our baby... You get to feel it every day, but me, today was...It's the most amazing feeling." He places his hand on my belly. "That's us in there, you and me. We did that. I'm in awe of this entire fucking experience," he explains.

I run my fingers through his hair. "I know, babe. Me too." Before he can respond, the tech comes in.

"All right, Mr. and Mrs. MacCoy, are you ready to see your baby?" she asks as she pulls up my gown and places cold gel against my skin.

"You have no idea," Liam replies. I just nod my head yes and smile at her. I'm too excited to speak.

She hits a few buttons on the machine, and then gently rests the wand against my belly. Immediately, the screen fills with a three dimensional image of our peanut. The heartbeat is coming through the speakers loud and strong. Liam is clutching my hand, holding it against his lips. I can't stop the tears from flowing. My only indication that Liam is in as much awe I am is the grip he has on my hand. I cannot tear my eyes away from the screen.

The tech takes her time going over all the facial features, ten fingers, ten toes. Then she asks the question, "We're you wanting to know the sex?"

"Yes," Liam and I say in unison. No hesitation from either of us. We want to know if there is lots of blue or pink in our future.

She moves the wand and jiggles my belly around a little. This causes the baby to switch positions. "There." She points to the screen. "Congratulations, it's a girl," she tells us.

I hear a sob come from Liam, which causes me to break my gaze away from our daughter and check on my husband. He's crying and wearing the biggest smile I've ever seen. He must feel me watching him, because he leans down and kisses my lips. "Another beautiful girl to steal my heart," he whispers.

The tech continues to roll over my belly and show us different angles of our daughter. Once she's finished, she wipes off my belly and tells me she is going to step out so I can get dressed and our package should be ready soon. I assume by package she means pictures. I heard Liam ask about taking sonogram pictures home when he signed us in.

Liam picks me up off the table bridal style and spins us in a circle around the room. "We're having a girl." he cheers. I'm sure the entire facility now knows. I don't bother to scold him. He's happy. We're happy.

As I walk out of the small bathroom from changing, the tech is back with a bag she is handing to Liam. "Congrats to both of you." With that, she turns and walks out of the room.

"Hey, baby, are you ready to go?" his smile and excitement is contagious.

"Yes, Daddy. Let's go spread the word," I tell him.

"A baby girl," he says reverently.

I smile. I love this man. "What's in the bag?" I motion toward his hands.

"Oh, this is the package I bought. It's a video of the ultrasound so we can watch it and show everyone else. It's also a photo package. I told them I wanted the deluxe visit and everything that entailed. We have several copies of the picture of her face. We can give them to our family." He smiles.

Our family.

I have a family. I place my hands over our princess. This is my canvas and I'm throwing as much color at it as I can. Live and Love Fearless.

Chapter Forty-Four

H ailey

The last two days have been amazing. Aiden and I turned our phones off, tuning out the outside world, and just worked on us and spent time together. I questioned and he said Liam knew where we were and if they needed to get ahold of us, they could. I felt better knowing our family could reach us if there was an emergency. I always have my phone on, but I have to admit, going unplugged with my husband is something I hope we do again.

We check out early and head home. There are a few jobs I was supposed to send resumes to and I don't want to miss the deadline. It's not that I have to work; I just want to. Aiden will be gone a lot when the season starts, and it will give me something to do. He says I could travel with him, but I know Allison will not be able to travel at that point in her pregnancy, so I've decided to stay home.

Once in the car headed home, I turn on both of our cell phones. As soon as they boot up, both of them ping with alerts like crazy. I scroll through my texts. Allison and Liam both messaged me to call them.

There are two missed calls from my mom and Aiden's. "Check mine will you, babe?" Aiden asks me.

I pick up his phone and the same thing, texts and phone calls from all of them. "Same thing. I hope everyone is okay," I say as I hit Allison's number. I place my phone on speaker so Aiden will be able to hear the conversation.

"Finally." she says in greeting.

"Hey, Allie. Aiden and I went unplugged for a few days," I explain.

"Oh, I know. Liam told me, but we were hoping you would check your messages. Where are you?" she asks. I can hear the excitement in her voice.

"We just left the Ritz. Why? Is everything okay?" I ask, concerned.

"Yes, it's perfect. Why don't you guys stop here for a few minutes before you head home? Liam and I have something we want to show you."

I turn to look at Aiden and he nods yes. "Okay, we'll be there in about fifteen minutes," I tell her.

"Great." she says and the line goes dead.

"I wonder what that's all about?" She sounded really happy, so I feel confident that everyone is okay.

"I don't know. Maybe they worked on the nursery or something and want to show us." Aiden shrugs.

"I think I'll wait until after we leave their house to call our moms back," I tell him.

"Probably a good idea. You know how they like to talk." He winks at me.

My heart is so full. I feel like a huge weight has been lifted from my shoulders. Aiden loves me regardless. I've know that all along; I was just too stupid to block out the negative thoughts. I've learned my lesson. Communication is a huge factor in a successful marriage, any relationship. I learned that the hard way. I'm thankful I married an amazing man.

Aiden pulls into the drive and we get out of the car. Liam and Allison are standing on the front porch waiting for us. Both of them are wearing blinding smiles.

"Hey," I say, giving Allison a hug and rubbing her baby bump. She looks amazing pregnant.

I move on to my big brother giving him a hug. "You good?" he whispers low enough for just us.

"More than good. He's amazing," I reply.

Liam nods like he knows exactly what I'm saying. I know Aiden talked to him about what was going on. I'm grateful we all have each other.

Liam and Aiden do the man hug, hand shake business and we all go inside. "So what's up?" Aiden asks them.

"Well," Allison says, "Liam scheduled us an appointment at Becoming Mom—"

"Gimme, gimme," I say, holding out my hand, interrupting her. She laughs at me.

"We have pictures for you, but first we want you to watch it," Liam says as he leads us into the living room.

Aiden plops down on the couch and pulls me onto his lap. Liam and Allison are in a similar situation, only they are in a recliner. "New chair?" I ask them.

"Yeah, I have trouble sleeping, especially when Liam's not here. Some of the forums I'm on say that sleeping in a recliner helps.

Liam points the remote at the flat screen and the sound of their baby's heartbeat pounds through the surround sound. I watch, my eyes glued to the screen, as different shots of the baby flash on the screen. I don't realize I'm crying until I feel Aiden wipe the tears from my cheeks.

"That's amazing," I choke out through my tears.

"And," Liam starts, "we found out what we're having," he says.

Instead of continuing on to tell us, he just smiles down at the love of his life. "Enough already. I can't take it. Tell me." I scold them.

Liam looks at Allison as if asking if she wants to tell us. "Go ahead," she tells him.

"It's a girl," Liam says softly, never taking his eyes off his wife. "We're having a baby girl."

I'm on my feet, pulling both of them into a hug. I feel Aiden behind me. Joining in the celebration, he wraps his arms around all of us.

Liam hands me a frame; inside is a close up sonogram of my niece's face.

Aiden, who is standing behind me, tilts the frame so he can see. "She's going to have us wrapped around her little finger," He says, staring at the frame.

"Just like her momma," Liam replies.

Chapter Forty-Five

L iam

This is the second week of training camp and it sucks ass. I miss my wife. I miss sleeping next to her. I miss feeling my daughter kick my palm. I just fucking miss them. I love my job, but being away from Allison is worse this time around. Last year, we were engaged and I missed her, but fuck, I don't remember it like this. I talked to Dad the other night and mentioned it to him. He said if it's anything like him and Mom, he falls more in love with her every day. I agree with him. It still sucks.

At least Aiden's here. We have two hours a day in between practices and meetings that they call free time. It's bullshit really. I'm not free to go home and see my wife, but I can call her. I can also catch up with my best friend. Aiden is having just as hard of a time with this as I am. He and Hales just got things on track before we left. He's worried the distance will set them back.

We're just about to start the second practice of the day when Coach calls me to the sidelines. "MacCoy, I need you to hit the lockers and change out of your uniform. Make it fast," He tells me.

"Coach?" I ask in confusion.

"MacCoy, are you questioning my judgment?" he seethes.

"No, sir," I say as I sprint off to the locker rooms to change out of my gear. I rack my brain as to why he wants me to do this. It's training camp and I'm the fucking QB. I'm supposed to be on the field with my team.

I'm back in gym shorts and a t-shirt in no time. When I open the locker room door, my dad is standing there and my heart stops. "Where is she?" I ask immediately.

"Let's get you in the car, and then I will explain," Dad says as he turns and runs out of the stadium. His car is parked out front. I climb in, slamming the door.

"Tell me what happened? Where is she?"

He pulls out into traffic. "When your mother got there today to check on her, she didn't answer the door. Your mom used her key to get into the house. She called out for her, but she didn't answer." He swallows. "She found her in your bathroom on the floor. Your mom said her hair was wet and it looked like she had just gotten out of the shower and fell."

"Oh, God." My stomach churns and I feel like I'm going to be sick, but I don't tell him. He has to keep driving; he has to get me to Allie.

"Your mom called 911 and then she called me. I called the stadium and explained what was going on. They patched me through to your coach and here we are. I called the Emersons' and Hailey on my way here. Your coach has assured me that as soon as practice is over, he will excuse Aiden from the meetings and give him a pass to meet us at the hospital."

"Is she hurt? Was she conscious? The baby? How's the baby? You said she fell, did she hit her belly?" I fire off questions that I know he doesn't have the answers to.

"I don't know, son. They won't give us any information. We are not her parents and neither are the Emersons'. You're the only person they will talk to. The only thing they will tell us is that Allison and the baby are both stable. We will have to wait until we get you there to learn anything more."

"Fuck." I scream. I lean down and place my elbows on my knees, knitting my fists in my hair. It's then that I pray to anyone who will listen—God, her parents, her Gran. I pray for them to keep her safe, to keep our baby safe.

Dad pulls up outside of the ER door and I'm out of the car before he comes to a complete stop. I run up the steps and slide to a halt at the counter. "Allison MacCoy," I say her name, fighting back the sobs that are threatening to break free.

The receptionist looks up and I see recognition cross her face. "Yes, Mr. MacCoy, I will let the doctor know you are here," she tells me.

"I want to see my wife," I grit.

"Yes, sir, let me just get the doctor," she says again. I know this chick is just trying to do her job, but I'm about to come un-fucking-glued.

"Now. Take me to my wife, now." I yell at her. I feel a hand tug on my arm. Looking down, I see the tear stained cheeks of my mother. I wrap my arms around her just as my sobs break free. "Why won't they let me see her?" I ask through my tears.

"Mr. MacCoy?" I hear a deep voice behind me. "I'm Dr. Wallace. Follow me please and I can fill you in on your wife and baby." He turns to walk toward a door labeled "Private."

I fall into step behind him. My mom right behind me. "Mr. MacCoy, your wife is stable as is your baby. Your wife has a condition called preeclampsia. One of the symptoms is dizziness. Allison said she felt faint when getting out of the shower. She fell and hit her head. She has a nasty bump, but she's lucky. We are monitoring the baby closely with a fetal monitor. Your wife's obstetrician has also been in to see her. He performed an ultrasound to ensure that your baby is healthy."

"Thank God, when can I see her," I ask him.

"I can take you to her. Mr. MacCoy, preeclampsia is a serious medical condition that can harm both your wife and your baby. Her blood pressure is extremely high. I know her obstetrician will round again this evening. We are admitting her overnight for observation."

"Thank you, now can I see my wife?" I ask. I try to remain calm. I don't know why these people don't understand that I need to see her.

"This way," he says.

Finally.

"We can only allow two in at a time until we get her in a room," he explains.

"Liam, I'm going to go update your father, Hales, and the Emersons'. You go on ahead and check on our girl. We will come back one at a time after we give you a few minutes," Mom says.

My mom. She knows me. She knows I won't leave her.

The doctor leads me to her room. I thank him for everything and take a deep breath before opening her door. I make my way to the bed, grabbing her hand and bringing it to my lips for a kiss. She's hooked up to a ton of machines. Leaning down, I kiss his forehead next to the bruise. As I sit in the chair beside her bed, her eyes flutter open.

"Liam," she says, her voice weak.

"Shh, baby. I'm here." I gently stroke the hair out of her eyes. "I was so scared, Allison. I thought I was losing both of you."

"They said the baby, she's okay," she explains.

"Yeah, you are both going to be okay. You have preeclampsia, which is high blood pressure; at least that's how the ER doc explained it."

"Yeah, my OB was in just before you. He said they are keeping me overnight for observation for both the sake of me and the baby. They are moving me to the maternity floor. He said there is a pretty good chance I will be on bed rest for the remainder of my pregnancy," she tells me.

"Whatever keeps you both safe and healthy, that's what we will do."

"Are you in trouble for being here?"

Amazingly, she's the one in the hospital bed and she's worried about me being in trouble. "No, Coach sent me. I don't know how long I will be allowed to stay. They are giving Aiden a pass for tonight."

I lean up and kiss her forehead. "Rest, baby. They will be moving you to a room soon. I'll be right here when you wake up." I can see she's exhausted. I know she hasn't been sleeping well.

Fuck. I know Coach is going to make me come back. How do I leave Allie and the baby? She can't be on her own and be on bed rest. This is tearing me up inside.

Chapter Forty-Six

iden

I watched Coach call Liam to the sidelines and then he took off toward the locker room. I kept waiting for him to come back, but he never did. When I questioned Coach he said he had him working on a special play. What the hell?

Practice sucked ass. The heat is excruciating and our backup QB has nothing on Liam. I make my way off the field. I'm going to give Liam shit for this one. How the hell did he rate to "work on a special play" while the rest of us melt and have to deal with the backup QB who needs to study some plays himself.

"Emerson." Coach yells. I turn and walk back to the field toward him. "Take a seat, son," he says as he points to the bench on the sidelines.

What the hell is going on? "Listen, I got a call right as practice was starting that MacCoy's wife was being rushed to the hospital. I lied to you to keep your head in the game. You have a free pass tonight to join your family. I expect you back here bright and early in the morning," he says. "I just talked to Liam's dad and Allison and the baby are both fine. Drive safe, son," he says, patting me on the back.

I sit in shock for a few minutes before I haul ass to the showers. I try calling Hales, but she doesn't answer. I'm sure she has her phone off if she is at the hospital. Shit, please let them both be okay.

On the way to the hospital, my dad calls to tell me Allison and the baby are both stable and they are keeping her overnight for observation. He says they have just moved her to the maternity floor into a private room. This is where I find everyone a few minutes later when I arrive. Hailey spots me and runs into my arms. God, I missed her. I hate that I'm seeing my wife under these circumstances, but holy hell, she feels good in my arms.

"Have you seen her yet?" I ask as I hold her tight against me. I don't have to be back until the morning and I don't plan on letting her out of my sight until then.

"Yeah, we've all been in. Liam hasn't left her side."

I can only imagine what he's going through.

"Can I talk to you?" Hailey asks quietly.

I nod and pull her into the corner of the waiting area. I hug her close one more time before releasing her. "What's up, angel?" She looks worried.

"I was thinking, maybe I will put off looking for a job for now. Allison is going to be on bed rest more than likely for the remainder of her pregnancy. With two weeks left of training camp and then the season starting...she can't be alone." She pauses as she stares out the window. "I want to stay with her, take care of her. I'm a neonatal nurse. I've delivered babies. She needs me, Aiden." Her voice cracks.

"Baby, I think that is the best idea you have ever had. I know Liam is going crazy right now, worrying about her being alone. You have the qualifications and you're family. You're amazing, Hailey Emerson."

She blushes at my praise. "I just want to help them."

"Why don't we go back and run the idea by them?" I suggest.

Hailey laces her fingers though mine and leads me to Allison's room. Liam is sitting beside the bed with one hand on her belly the other pressed against his lips. Allison is sleeping peacefully.

"Hey," he says when he hears us walk in. We make small talk about practice. I tell him how his backup can't hold a candle to him. He tells us that Allie and the baby are both stable and they are keeping her for twenty-four hour observation to watch them both.

Hailey tells him her plan how she wants to take over Allison's care so he can focus on the League and rest easy that she will have family with her twenty-four seven. As soon as she finishes with her idea, my best friend drops his shoulders and sobs. It's hard to see a six foot four tank break down.

He stands up and walks across the room. He lifts Hailey in his arms and hugs her tight. "I love you, sis." I hear his gruff voice and I have to swallow back my own tears. "I was so worried about what I was going to do. I was going to hire a private nurse, but I knew Allie would hate that. I thought about asking you, but I didn't want you to feel obligated."

"Hailey Emerson, get your ass over here and give me a hug," Allison says in a sleepy voice. Hailey is at her side in an instant. "Thank you. I just...thank you. I know this will be a burden on you."

"Actually, it will keep me busy. I have only sent out a few resumes, and with Aiden being gone, that house is lonely. We will be helping each other," she tells Allison.

I breathe a sigh of relief that the girls will be together. I worry about Hales and Allison both staying all alone when we are gone so much. This eliminates more than just Liam's worries. I know my parents and Liam's will be hovering over the girls as well. This is another relief. Liam and I don't have a choice but to leave due to the careers we have chosen. It helps us do our jobs knowing our families have our backs.

Chapter Forty-Seven

A llison

Two weeks, that's how long it's been since I have seen my husband. Two weeks since I have been home from the hospital. Liam's coach gave him a pass for the day I was released, but he had to go back after that. I've been spending my days on the couch and in my recliner. Hailey has been amazing. She caters to me and takes my vitals every few hours like the doctor instructed. Liam and Aiden's moms have been cooking us meals and bringing them by. All are based on my strict high blood pressure diet. I've read a lot. My Kindle and I have become reacquainted these past two weeks. Hailey and I watch TV, and she gave me a pedicure last night. She tries her best to keep me entertained. She also gives me my space. She doesn't hover and I love her face for that simple fact.

Today, however, Hailey seems distracted. I can tell something is on her mind. "You okay?" I ask her as she brings in a tray of fresh vegetables for us to snack on.

"Yeah," she says, biting her lip.

"Hales, spill it. Humor your bedridden sister-in-law." I welcome the distraction. I worry every day about our little princess. I had an appointment with my OB yesterday and he assured me that all is well and I should continue doing what I'm doing. I have an amazing nurse, what can I say?

"I'm late," she blurts out.

"Late, how late?" I ask her.

"A week. I can't bring myself to buy a test. I just don't want another disappointment."

"You don't need to buy one. Liam bought cases of the damn things when we were trying. They're upstairs in our bathroom closet. I'm sure they will expire before we need them again," I tell her.

She smirks at me. "Not if my brother can help it. He wants his own damn football team," she teases.

I laugh. She's right, we both do. "Okay, so you have a point, but still. Go upstairs and take one. Hell, take five." I laugh, waving my hands toward the steps. "I'll be here waiting."

Hailey hugs me and then dashes up the stairs. I pick up my Kindle and continue reading. Not three minutes later, I hear a scream and heavy footsteps on the stairs.

I lift my head to see Hailey come barreling into the living room. Her face is covered in tears, but it's lit up from her smile. "Positive," she says, holding up the test.

I go to stand and she scolds me. The next thing I know, she's on the floor kneeling in front of me and we are both hugging and crying. "I'm going to be an aunt." I say, excited. More family.

"Are you going to wait until they come home tomorrow to tell him?" I ask her.

"I...I don't really know. I guess, yeah. I don't want to tell him over the phone. How should I do it?"

"Well, I didn't have to worry about that. Liam found out I was late and hauled my ass up to the bathroom and stood outside the door. He wanted to stay in there with me. I refused." I laugh remember his excitement.

"Only Liam," she laughs.

"I know the guys both plan on coming straight here tomorrow. Why don't you make the same meal I did when we told the parents and see if he or Liam says anything," I suggest.

"That's perfect." She claps her hands together.

"I also have an 'I love my daddy' bib up in the room next to yours. That's going to be up in the nursery. I bought it a few weeks ago; I just couldn't resist. You can use that as your backup in case he doesn't figure it out."

Hailey plops down on the couch beside me. In her hand, she still clutches onto the positive pregnancy test. "I took three," she says with a smile. I did them all at the same time. I knocked the other two onto the bathroom floor when I reached for one to show you. I'm gonna have a baby," she says, her voice filled with awe.

I lean over and give her a hug. "And I'm going to be an aunt. I love you, Hales."

"Love you too, Allie."

Chapter Forty-Eight

H^{ailey}

I called Mom and asked her if she could come and sit with Allison for a few hours. I told her I needed to go to the store and stock up on food before the guys came home. She was all too happy to help. I don't want to tell her yet, not until I tell Aiden. Allison knows, but that's different.

I rushed back home and unloaded everything. I made sure I bought the exact meal. I did, however, pick up the cupcakes from the bakery. The guys get home around four and I didn't want to cut it close on time. Mom asked what the plans were and Allison saved my ass, big time.

"Oh, nothing really. Liam is so worried about me, he said he just wants a quiet night in," she tells her. It's not exactly a lie. She doesn't need to know that Aiden and I will be staying the night as well. Liam asked if we would. Of course, we said yes. Mom finally left with the promise to call tomorrow to see what time we could all get together. Allison promised to discuss it with Liam. I love that girl.

As soon as she left I started cooking. Allison wrapped the bib for me. I'm so excited to tell Aiden. To think about all we went through. I was willing to leave him, convinced this would never happen for us, but here we are. I don't think I've stopped smiling since I found out. Luckily, Mom just chalked it up to seeing my husband for the first time in weeks. I love it when a good plan comes together.

Allison and I are sitting on the couch, her feet propped up with the laptop between us. We're shopping online for ideas for her baby girl's nursery. Of course, she won't make a final decision without Liam. If I know my brother, she's going to have a princess room. It's still hard to believe that two years ago he wanted nothing to do with commitment. Love will do that to ya.

The front doors open and I freeze. "Just breathe," Allison whispers.

Heavy footsteps tramp down the hall. The next thing I know, I'm being pulled up off the couch and Liam is taking my place. Aiden has me in a tight embrace with my feet dangling off the floor. "Hales," he says. Just hearing him say my name has my eyes filling with tears. "I missed you so fucking much."

Allison's laugh breaks us out of our trance. Aiden lets my feet slide to the floor, but he doesn't let go of me. We turn to see what's so funny and Liam has his head under her shirt, talking to the baby. I shake my head at my brother and his antics.

"Dinner is ready if you guys are hungry," I say. Might as well get this over with so I can calm the hell down.

They both grumble about being starved. Liam picks Allison up in his arms and carries her to the table. I pull out an extra chair and lay a pillow down so she can prop up her feet. I place a pillow behind her back as well. Liam kisses the top of her head, and then makes them both a plate. Aiden and I join them at the table a few minutes later.

We all dig in. Allison and I share a glance here and there, trying not to be obvious. It's Liam who speaks up first. "Baby, you didn't make this did you?" he turns to scowl at me.

"No, Liam. I used her recipe." I roll my eyes at him.

This gets my husband's attention. "This is the same meal we ate when…" Aiden stops and drops his fork on his plate. He closes his eyes, picks up his glass of tea, and takes a long drink.

"Yes, it is. Only this time, Hales cooked," Allison chimes in. I can see that Aiden wants to ask me if it's us, if we are having a baby. But after all we went through, I can tell he's afraid to.

Reaching over, I place my hand on his arm. He opens his eyes. "We're pregnant?" he asks hesitantly.

"Yes. Looks like we're going to learn how to do the parent thing," I reply.

He scoots back in his chair and it crashes to the floor. He reaches down and pulls me out of my chair and wraps his arms around me. He buries his face in my neck, breathing me in. "I love you so fucking much." His voice is thick with emotion. I don't respond. I can't. My tears are falling too fast for me to form a coherent sentence.

"Let me hug my sister," I hear Liam laugh behind us.

"No, go hug your own wife. I'm never letting go of mine," Aiden retorts.

I gently smack him on the back of the head. He chuckles and releases me and I'm swooped into another bear hug by my big brother. "Congrats, Hales. Our kids are going to grow up together," he says this so only I can hear.

Aiden goes to Allison since Liam gave her strict orders not to get up. Once all the hugs are passed out, we go back to dinner.

After dinner, the guys clean up the kitchen so their, and I quote, "Baby Mommas" can get off their feet. They must have been working with lighting speed, because ten minutes later they are joining us in the living room. I have a feeling they put the food away and stopped there. Oh well, we have not seen them in weeks, so as far as I'm concerned, the dishes can wait.

We discuss the season and how I will stay with Allison during all the away games and during home games. Both my mom and Aiden's will also be called in to help. Our husbands think, since I am also pregnant, I can't be overdoing it. We put our foot down at hiring a maid to come a few times a week. Allison and I, neither one, want that to be our lifestyle. We want to take care of our families.

Aiden and I tell them we are not going to tell our parents at least until after my first doctor's appointment. Liam told him that he had to take me to Becoming Mom. I can't help but smile as these two gentle giants carrying on a conversation about babies and fatherhood.

An hour later, Aiden stands up and announces we are going home for the night. Liam nods in understanding. I'm not sure why he felt like I needed to stay. I guess since he had not seen Allie since the day she was released, he was worried about how she would look and feel. She's doing great. Her blood pressure is still a little high, but the swelling is under control. She is very obedient as far as staying off her feet. She only gets up to shower and use the restroom. She will do anything to keep her baby safe.

We say our goodbyes and drive home. As soon as we are inside, Aiden secures the lock on the door and picks me up in his arms. He carries me upstairs and lays me on the bed. He kneels down beside the bed and lifts my shirt. He places his hand over my stomach, fingers spread wide. "We did it, Hales," he says softly. "We made a baby." He leans over and places a kiss right below my belly button.

He stands up and strips out of his clothes. He then helps me stand and takes off all of mine. I slide back into bed while Aiden turns out the light. He slides in next to me and pulls my back against his chest. He splays a protective hand over our baby. "I missed you," he says.

"I missed you too," I reply, but I can tell he is already half asleep. I place my hand over top of his and let sleep claim me.

Chapter Forty-Nine

Three Months Later

Liam

Fourth quarter, twenty seconds left on the clock. We're up by twelve points. We remain undefeated this season. Aiden and I are being referred to as the dream team. Hell, we've played together since college. Not only is he my best friend, but my brother-in-law as well. We are constantly together and discussing strategy and plays. We practically share a brain, at least that's what our wives tell us.

I watch as the time runs out and cheer with my teammates as we bring home another win. Just as I'm about to step out and shake hands with the other team, Coach yells for me. "MacCoy."

I turn around to see what he wants. He's holding the phone in his hand. "Just got a call from your dad. Allison's in labor. They want you to meet them at the hospital."

Labor? Shit, she's two weeks early. I rush to the locker room and start tearing off my uniform, all the while trying to get ahold of Dad on his cell. Finally, he picks up. "Hey, son, ready to meet your baby girl?" he asks.

"Dad, how is she. How's Allie?" I ask, frantic.

Dad chuckles. "She's fine, son. Her water broke and the contractions are still over ten minutes apart. You have plenty of time to get here. Make sure you have Aiden drive you," he tells me.

"Is she with you? Can I talk to her?" I ask, needing to hear her tell me she's okay.

"Liam," Allison's voice is cheerful on the other end. "We get to meet our little girl," she squeals into the phone.

Just hearing her voice helps me calm down. "You good, baby?" I ask her.

"Yes, no pain until a contraction and they are short and far apart, so right now, yes, I'm good. We'll meet you there," she says and the phone goes silent.

"I'm going to be a father." I jump back into action and whip off the rest of my gear. I take the world's fastest shower and throw on some clothes. I find Aiden waiting for me at my locker.

"Hey, Coach just told me. Have you talked to her?" he asks as he tears off his uniform.

"Yeah, she sounds happy. Her water broke and her contractions are still a good ways apart."

"Good, go. I'm just going to shower real fast and then I will be right behind you." He waves his hand as to push me out the door. I hesitate only for a minute. I'm a wreck, but I'm better since I talked to Allison. I don't want to wait on Aiden. I feel okay to drive.

When I reach my car in the players' lot, there is a county sheriff parked beside me. "Good game, son." he says. "Little birdie tells me you're about to have a baby. Hop in, I'll make sure you get there."

Not one to kick a gift horse in the mouth, I climbed in the cruiser. He turns on the lights and I am that much closer to Allie and our baby girl.

$$Chapter\ Fifty$$

A llison

The nurses keep telling me I am the most chipper woman in labor they have ever met. I don't bother telling them that today, another dream of mine comes true. Liam and I will welcome a new member to our little family. I wanted this baby. No way will you hear me whining about pain. Nope, not gonna happen.

Liam is sitting on the edge of my bed and he's all smiles too. I don't know who's more excited to meet our little girl. I got an epidural about an hour ago and now I feel no pain at all. I'm just laying here relaxing, talking to everyone. All eight of us are here to welcome her.

The nurse comes in to check on me and says it's go time. I'm surprised because I don't feel anything. There is a little pressure, but no pain. The next hour goes by so slowly. Liam and Hailey hold my legs while I push and push and push. I'm exhausted, but I refuse to give up. The doctor just said if we don't make any headway in the next couple of contractions, she will have to be delivered Caesarean. I don't want that to happen, so when he counts to three, I bear down as hard as I can and push with everything I have. Liam and Hailey are both grunting with me and telling me how great I'm doing. I don't yell at them. I know they're just trying to help. Finally, I hear the most precious sound, the cry of our baby girl.

Hailey excuses herself to tell everyone that we have a beautiful healthy baby girl. The nurse swaddles her in a blanket and lays her on my chest. I kiss her head. She's the most beautiful little girl I've ever seen.

Liam leans down and kisses me, then our daughter. Tears are running unchecked down his cheeks. "That was amazing; you're amazing. I love you so much."

I raise my hand and wipe at his tears. "I love you, too. Thank you for giving me this miracle." I kiss her one more time on the cheek. "Daddy, would you like to hold our daughter?" I ask him.

With a nod, Liam leans down and takes her from my arms. He pulls back the blanket and counts all ten fingers and ten toes. Her little hand grabs onto his finger and he smiles. "You already have my heart, princess," he says to her.

The doctor and nurses finish with me and leave us alone with our daughter. "Sophia," Liam says. We had yet to agree on a name, but Sophia was one on the list.

"I like that. I would also like her middle name to be Hailey. She did so much for us, taking care of me, and she's my best friend. None of this would even be possible if she had not introduced us." I wait for his reaction.

His smile lights up his face. "Sophia Hailey MacCoy."

I smile and nod, fighting back yet another round of tears. There is a knock at the door and in walks our family, Aiden and Hailey, followed by Aiden and Liam's parents. Liam places Sophia in my arms, and then sits next to us on the bed and puts his arm around me. He takes his free hand and gives a finger to baby Sophia. She grabs on with all of her might. "Everyone," Liam says, "I would like for you to meet our daughter. She's six pounds five ounces and nineteen inches long."

There are rounds of "She's beautiful" and "Congratulations." Then Hailey speaks up. "What's her name?"

I look to Liam and he nods for me to announce her name. I look right at Hailey. "Her name is Sophia Hailey MacCoy." I watch as surprise crosses her face, then wonder. "Would you like to hold her?" Hailey just nods yes. Liam takes Sophia from me and passes her on to Hales. After everyone has had a turn, they all leave with the promise to come back and visit the next day. I scoot over and pat the bed beside me.

"I don't want to hurt you," he says as he runs his fingers through my hair.

"You won't lay with us, Daddy?" I knew that would get him.

He smiles down at us and squeezes his big frame onto my bed. His arm is around me and Sophia is holding tightly to his finger.

This little girl and her daddy are my heart and soul. I will treasure every moment I have with them.

Chapter Fifty-One

Six Months Later

Aiden

Hailey and I are lounging around the house today. She's due to deliver our little man any day now, so I like for us to stay close to home, close to the hospital. We are sitting on the couch watching television; well, Hailey is watching television. I'm playing with my son. To this day, it still amazes me how he responds to my voice. If I get really close to her belly and talk, he kicks. I've even gently wiggled her belly around to wake him up, and then he really kicks like crazy. I love watching him move.

"Would you stop? The last time you got him all wound up, he kicked the hell out of my ribs."

I smile at my dear wife, who is miserable. Her due date was actually Monday. Today is Friday and she's not impressed. I feel bad for her. The doctor says that if her water does not break over the weekend, he will admit her and give her medication that will initiate the labor. Hales tried to convince him to do it yesterday at our appointment, but he wanted to give it a few more days.

"Ugh. I have to pee again."

I hop off the couch and extend my hand to help her up. She hates needing help. As soon as she stands up, she sucks in a deep breath. "Hales, what's wrong?" My first thought is I did something when I was playing with him. Maybe he worked himself into a spot that is extremely uncomfortable for her.

"Well, I either pissed my pants, or my water just broke."

I peer down and see that, indeed, her grey yoga pants are drenched. "Okay, baby, it's time. The bags are already in the car. Do you need anything else?" How I'm being so calm, I have no idea. I think it's because of the fear I see on Hailey's face.

She shakes her head no. I grab my keys and cell phone and lead her out to the car. Once we're on the road, I call Liam and ask him to let our parents know. He says he will take care of it and they will meet us at the hospital.

By the time we arrive at the ER, Hailey's contractions are two minutes apart. Our little man has decided today is the day. I explain to the nurse that her water broke at home and how close the contractions are. She immediately calls to the maternity floor and tells them to have the doctor on call ready and that we are on our way up.

The next thirty minutes are a whirlwind. As soon as we get to the maternity floor, Hailey screams in pain. A flurry of activity surrounds us as they change her into a gown and get IV in her arm. The house doctor comes in and checks her. "Hailey, your baby is crowning. There is not enough time to give you an epidural. I can give you something in your IV to help dull the pain, but it will not be nearly as effective as an epidural. I'm going to need you to push for me. Are you ready?" I hold one leg while a nurse holds the other. Hailey screams out in pain as she pushes with all she's got. The doctor praises her and tells her how well she's doing. "One more push," he tells her. I watch as she bears down and gives it everything she's got.

That's when I hear him cry. Hales collapses against the bed, drained. I lean down and kiss her lips. "You did it, angel. You're amazing. He's finally here," I say to her. The nurse brings our little man over and places him on Hailey's chest.

"Nine pounds and eleven ounces, twenty-two inches long," she rattles off his stats. I unwrap him and Hales counts his fingers while I count his toes. He's perfect. I remember how Sophia gripped Liam's finger as soon as she was born. I hold my finger next to his hand and he latches on. The little stinker has a good grip. My heart swells with love for my wife and my son.

Hailey bends down and kisses his cheek. "I love you, Henry Cole Emerson," she tells him. He stares at her, eyes wide open. Right now they are blue, though Hales says that's normal. I hope they don't change. I want him to have his momma's eyes. He's going to be a lady killer when he gets older.

Chapter Fifty-Two

H^{ailey}

Thirty minutes. That's how long it took from the time we walked through the Emergency Room doors until baby Henry was born. I'm thankful we made it here in time. I've read horror stories of women giving birth on the side of the highway. Last night, when everyone showed up, they were surprised to learn he was already here. They sat with us for about an hour or so, but I was exhausted, so they said their goodbyes.

I must have slept like a log because that's the last thing I remember. I know they gave me some pain medication that they claimed would make me sleepy. I feel bad that I didn't even wake for Henry. From the looks of things, Daddy has it all under control. Aiden is kicked back in the reclining chair that sits beside my bed. Henry is swaddled in his blanket, resting peacefully on his daddy's chest. I wish I had my camera or even my cell phone. I look over at the table and see Aiden's cell sitting there. I reach over as quietly and carefully as possible and snatch it. I swipe the screen and see a picture of me sleeping with Henry next to me. He must have staged it last night. It's already his screen saver. I hit the icon to pull up his camera. I check to make sure the sound is turned off and I snap a few pictures of the two of them. I text them to our parents as well as Liam and Allison.

Henry stirs and Aiden's eyes pop open. He looks at me and smiles. "Hey, Momma. Feeling better?"

"Yes, sorry I zoned out on you. It must have been the medication they gave me."

"Yeah, the nurse came in to check on the two of you a few times. She said the pain medication they put in your IV can cause deep sleep. You needed it though after all of your hard work bringing this little guy into the world," he says, kissing the top of Henry's head.

"You look like a pro."

"This little guy makes it easy. I can't get enough of him."

Aiden climbs out of the chair and I immediately scoot to the side of the bed, making room for my boys. He places Henry in my arms and puts his arm around my shoulder. "I love you, Hales. You are a strong, amazing, sexy momma who has made me the happiest man in the world. I never thought we could top our wedding day, but this is definitely a close second. I love our life. I can't wait to see what's in store for the next fifty years." He places a soft kiss against my lips.

My eyes are blurry as I fight back tears. "I thought we would never get here. Thank you for fighting for us, for me. You truly are my dream come true, Aiden Emerson."

Chapter Fifty-Three

S ix Years Later

Allison

Today is Sophia's sixth birthday. I cannot believe how fast time has flown by. She's growing up to be such a big girl. She's my little helper with her brothers. As we all knew she would be, she's Daddy's little princess. I swear she has Liam wrapped so tight around that little finger of hers. He says there is no way he can say no to her when she has eyes just like her momma.

Liam and I are as close as ever, nearly seven years of marriage and three kids later. I told him this morning that we are expecting number four. He's such an amazing father. I got pregnant with the boys when Sophia was thirteen months old. Due to my high risk pregnancy with Sophia, they brought me in for an ultrasound right away. It was then that they informed us that there was not only one little peanut but two, twins. Ross and Owen gave me a run for my money. I felt like I was as big as a house. I had issues with swelling and was put on bed rest near the end, but it was more because of my small frame and the two minia-ture linebackers I was carrying. The doctors were worried about me going into early labor, so bed rest it was. I just found out last night about this one. They had an away game, and the kids and I stayed home to watch it on TV. Hailey and the boys came over to watch it with us. She kept an eye on the kiddos while I slipped away to take the test. She laughed when I told her it was positive, and said Liam wouldn't stop until we had our own little MacCoy football team. I think she's right. Even Princess Sophia can throw a mean spiral for a five-year-old.

I step out onto the porch, and as if he feels my presence, my husband stops chasing our kids to look at me. He smiles and blows me a kiss just as the twins both grab a leg and try to take him down. Sophia comes along and helps her brothers. They all fall to the ground, laugh-ing, enjoying life. Gran's words come back to me: Live and Love Fear-less. That's exactly what we're doing every single day.

Chapter Fifty-Four

H ailey

I am seriously out-numbered in the Emerson household. The three to one ratio is just not cutting it, especially when my husband fits in so well with our four-and-a-half-year-old and our two-year-old. Henry and Jaxon are currently chasing their dad with the water hose on the back deck. They know Sophia's party starts in an hour. I have reminded them and their father several times. Even though they are a handful, all three of them hold my heart. My baby boys are so much like their daddy; they mimic everything he does. Case in point, last week, Henry smacked me on the ass as I was walking out of the living room. When I asked him why, he said in his cutest four-year-old voice, "Daddy does it; why can't I?" Of course, when I told Aiden about it, he wanted to give him a high five and tell him good job. Again, I am way outnumbered.

We're trying for baby number three. Allison keeps telling me it's our turn to have twins. They don't run in our family, so I'm not worried. I don't really care what number three turns out to be. Boy or girl, I will love them the same. Yes, a little girl would be great help to even things out a little. I think it would be good for Aiden as well. He is constantly giving Liam hell about Sophia when she gets old enough to date. At five, she is a looker. I can only imagine what she will look like as a teenager. Aiden needs a little reality check, a step outside of the "boys" club, if you will.

Either way, we are blessed. We have two healthy little boys who are our world, and Aiden and I...we're solid. We learned early on in our marriage that it takes work and sacrifice and a hell of a lot of love. We have excelled at it and I can only hope we pass that on to our boys. Fight for who and what you love. Love with fierce determination, and always follow your heart.

Thank you

Thank you for taking the time to read Everything with You.

* * *

_Never miss a new release:__Newsletter Sign-up Be the first to hear about free content, new releases, cover reveals, sales, and more.

* * *

Discover more about Kaylee's books here.

* * *

Start the Riggins Brothers Series for FREE. Download Play by Play now.

Start the Kinciad Brothers Series for FREE. Download Stay Always now.

* * *

Contact Kaylee Ryan:
Website
Facebook
Instagram
Reader Group
Goodreads
BookBub
TikTok

More from Kaylee Ryan

With You Series:
Anywhere with You | More with You
Everything with You

Soul Serenade Series:
Emphatic | Assured
Definite | Insistent

Southern Heart Series:
Southern Pleasure | Southern Desire
Southern Attraction | Southern Devotion

Unexpected Arrivals Series
Unexpected Reality |Unexpected Fight
Unexpected Fall | Unexpected Bond
Unexpected Odds

Riggins Brothers Series:
Play by Play / Layer by Layer
Piece by Piece / Kiss by Kiss
Touch by Touch | Beat by Beat

Standalone Titles:

Tempting Tatum | Unwrapping Tatum | Levitate
Just Say When | I Just Want You
Reminding Avery
Hey, Whiskey
Pull You Through
Remedy | The Difference
Trust the Push | Forever After All
Misconception | Never with Me

Entangled Hearts Duet:
Agony | Bliss

Cocky Hero Club:
Lucky Bastard

Mason Creek Series:
Perfect Embrace

The Kissing Games Series:
Kissing the Rival

The Everlasting Ink Series:
Does He Know? / Is This Love?

Out of Reach Series:
Beyond the Bases / Beyond the Game
Beyond the Play /

Kincaid Brothers Series:
Stay Always / Stay Over
Stay Forever / Stay Tonight
Stay Together / Stay Wild

Co-written with Lacey Black:

Fair Lakes Series:

It's Not Over | Just Getting Started
Can't Fight It

Standalone Titles:

Boy Trouble
Home to You
Beneath the Fallen Stars
Tell Me A Story

www.ingramcontent.com/pod-product-compliance
Lightning Source LLC
Chambersburg PA
CBHW020438180626
46812CB00003B/1289